P9-DKD-951

"We should get married."

"What?" Jenny asked, as though he were speaking a language she didn't comprehend.

"We should get married."

"I don't want or need to get married. This is my life, my very own perfectly contented life, and believe me, Matthew Robert Hanson, you are not in it."

"Why?" he persisted.

"Would you please leave?"

"Miss Ames. Jenny." In what Matthew hoped was a soothing gesture, he rubbed the pad of his thumb across the pale, silky skin of her hand. With her hand in his, he felt a connection, a jolt of something unexpected. Did she feel the surge of electricity that shot through him and nearly made his heart stop beating?

Why did he have the eerie feeling that she, and everything about her, including the baby inside her, was meant to be his?

Dear Reader,

What are your favorite memories of summer? Even though I spend my days reading manuscripts, I love nothing better than basking in the sun's warm glow as I sit immersed in a great book. If you share this pleasure with me, rest assured that I can make packing your beach bag *really* easy this month!

Certainly, you'll want to make room in your bag for Patricia Thayer's *A Taste of Paradise* (SR #1770), part of the author's new LOVE AT THE GOODTIME CAFÉ miniseries. Thayer proves that romance is the order of the day when a sexy sheriff determined to buy back his family's ranch crosses paths with a beautiful blond socialite who is on the run from an arranged marriage. Watch the sparks fly in *Rich, Rugged...Royal* by Cynthia Rutledge (SR #1771) in which an ordinary woman discovers that the man whom she had a one-night affair with is not only her roommate but also a royal! International bestselling author Lilian Darcy offers an emotional tale about an estranged couple who are reunited when the hero is named bachelor of the year, in *The Millionaire's Cinderella Wife* (SR #1772). Finally, I'm delighted to introduce you to debut author Karen Potter whose *Daddy in Waiting* (SR #1773) shows how a mix-up at a fertility clinic leads to happily ever after.

And be sure to leave some room in your bag next month when Judy Duarte kicks off a summer-themed continuity set at a county fair!

Happy reading,

Ann Leslie Tuttle
Associate Senior Editor

Please address questions and book requests to:
Silhouette Reader Service
U.S.: 3010 Walden Ave., P.O. Box 1325, Buffalo, NY 14269
Canadian: P.O. Box 609, Fort Erie, Ont. L2A 5X3

Daddy in Waiting

KAREN POTTER

SILHOUETTE *Romance*®

Published by Silhouette Books

America's Publisher of Contemporary Romance

If you purchased this book without a cover you should be aware
that this book is stolen property. It was reported as "unsold and
destroyed" to the publisher, and neither the author nor the
publisher has received any payment for this "stripped book."

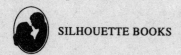

SILHOUETTE BOOKS

ISBN 0-373-19773-X

DADDY IN WAITING

Copyright © 2005 by Karen Potter

All rights reserved. Except for use in any review, the reproduction
or utilization of this work in whole or in part in any form by any
electronic, mechanical or other means, now known or hereafter
invented, including xerography, photocopying and recording, or in
any information storage or retrieval system, is forbidden without
the written permission of the editorial office, Silhouette Books,
233 Broadway, New York, NY 10279 U.S.A.

All characters in this book have no existence outside the imagination of
the author and have no relation whatsoever to anyone bearing the same
name or names. They are not even distantly inspired by any individual
known or unknown to the author, and all incidents are pure invention.

This edition published by arrangement with Harlequin Books S.A.

® and TM are trademarks of Harlequin Books S.A., used under license.
Trademarks indicated with ® are registered in the United States Patent
and Trademark Office, the Canadian Trade Marks Office and in other
countries.

Visit Silhouette Books at www.eHarlequin.com

Printed in U.S.A.

KAREN POTTER

Librarian by day, romance writer by night and dreamer 24/7, Karen is often surprised at how deeply and completely her characters fall in love. She is a longtime seeker of happily-ever-after, and hopes it will always be that way.

A transplanted Kentuckian currently living in Florida, Karen finds sunshine to be more conducive to writing than the knee-high snows she remembers from childhood. While she misses the changing seasons, she finds that being able to sit outside and read year-round more than makes up for it.

You can visit Karen at her Web site
www.karen-potter.com or write to her at
P.O. Box 196962, Winter Springs, Florida 32719-6962.

This book is dedicated to Teresa Elliott Brown,
Katherine Garbera and Patricia Waddell.
Thank you for your support and encouragement and for
always saying the right thing just when I needed to hear it.

And for Thunder.
We did it, little bug.

Chapter One

What would her great-grandmother say about her decision to have a baby without snagging a husband first?

Jenny Ames turned the squeaky swivel chair to face the window and squinted into the bright sunlight of a perfect fall Cincinnati day. Spotting the cloud she suspected held her great-grandmother's restless spirit, she sighed.

The grand old lady, gone for nearly ten years, haunted Jenny still. She'd fussed about Jenny's posture, the clothes she wore, the foods she ate, the friends she chose.

Jenny grinned. Grandmother would have had a double coronary at the first mention of the words *sperm bank* anyway, so everything after that would have been a waste of breath.

Too bad she'd never know her great-great-grandchild.

As for her own parents, Jenny gave only a fleeting thought. They were probably too busy bed hopping across the Australian outback in the guise of documentary filmmakers to be curious about her baby.

If Jenny had told them about the baby.

Which she hadn't. They didn't know the first thing about loving or protecting a child anyway, so why bother? She and Alexis would be a family of two, and they would be the happiest family the world had ever seen. Jenny had learned from experts what *not* to do, and she was determined never again to place her happiness in someone else's hands.

Pulled from her musings by the opening of the office door, Jenny's gaze went to the tall, tanned man who entered. Brown hair, brown eyes, irresistible as a chocolate bar. An unfamiliar thrill tore through her, but she fought it. Seven-and-then-some months pregnant was not the time to be getting swept away by strange, albeit handsome, men.

His overabundance of sex appeal was clothed to perfection in an Armani suit and he carried a briefcase made from the skin of some unfortunate reptile. Jenny wondered if he'd wrestled it down himself. His dark eyes showed no emotion; not pleasure, not welcome, not a spark of friendliness. The solid set of his jaw bespoke a mild annoyance. He looked wealthy, confident and determined. Very determined.

Jenny felt instantly intimidated. They seldom had unexpected visitors at the Prescott Foundation. Although the nameplate on her office door said Executive Director, today she wore the receptionist hat. In the two-person office, both she and her assistant changed hats often, never caring how the arrangement looked to the outside world as long as the job got done.

She straightened her back and arranged the jacket of

her prim business suit to cover her belly. She smiled. He didn't.

"May I help you?" she asked.

"I'm here to see Genevieve Marie Ames," he said brusquely. "Is she in?"

Jenny suppressed a shiver of fear. Who was this serious and unsettling man and what did he want with her?

"Is she?" he repeated.

"Excuse me, is she what?"

"Is Miss Ames in?"

Ah, reprieve.

"I'm sorry. Miss Ames is not in her office." Well, technically she wasn't, but he didn't need to know that. She shrugged, excusing her little white lie. "Would you like to leave a message?"

As she reached for a pad and pencil, the lapels of her jacket fell away to reveal her belly. Tall, dark and dangerous leaned forward to offer his card. His hand froze in midair as his eyes made contact with the very visible evidence of her pregnancy.

Jenny had been stared at before. Most pregnant women were fair game for the leerers of the world, but never before had she been looked at with such possession. It was like being touched by invisible hands...only much more frightening.

The office door opened, and from the corner of her eye Jenny saw her assistant breeze in.

"I've got to run to the mail room, but then I'll be back, Jenny," she heard Nancy shout.

"Jenny? Would that be short for Genevieve, by any chance?"

"Who are you?" Jenny asked.

"My name is Matt Hanson." He released the business

card and it fluttered to the desk. He pointed a slender finger at her belly.

"And I believe that's my baby."

Matt watched without satisfaction as what little color in Jenny Ames's face drained away. She was pale anyway, with her platinum-blond hair and soft-blue eyes, but if she'd had any color left over from the hot summer just past, it was gone now. He felt a momentary concern that she might faint, but then again she wouldn't be the first person to meet the floor facefirst over this situation.

She rose slowly and indicated the foundation's conference room with a delicate gesture of her small, trembling hand. "Perhaps we should speak privately."

Once through the door she walked to a window at the far side of the room. Matt took a position by the door, barring both entrance and exit.

In the minutes before she spoke, he had an opportunity to study the woman who'd unwittingly turned his life upside down. He'd always scoffed when people talked about how pregnant women glowed, yet Jenny Ames was the epitome of maternal beauty.

Her hair was pulled back into a knot at the nape of her slender neck, and her plain blue suit was a perfect complement to the seriousness of her position at the foundation. With her full breasts and rounded belly it was difficult to imagine what she'd looked like before, but he'd bet his last dime she'd been a knockout.

She appeared serene and conservative, grace under fire, a woman any man would be happy to have on his arm, pregnant or not…and sexy…damned sexy, if the messages his body was sending him were to be believed.

Matt warned himself to get a grip. He watched as she

turned toward him, swallowed nervously and licked her soft, pink lips. She assessed his appearance as he'd assessed hers. A strong believer in fair being fair, he didn't protest. There was nothing in her expression that telegraphed appreciation, but at least she didn't gag.

Resting one hand atop her belly she met his gaze and asked not *Where have you been all my life?* but "Could you tell me your name again, please?"

Oh, well, so much for that flash of recognition he'd always expected from the woman who would bear his child.

"Hanson. Matthew Robert Hanson."

"Do I know you?"

"No, Miss Ames. We've never met."

"Then why do you think the child I'm carrying is yours?"

"You know Dr. Horace Bentley at the Morningstar Clinic, I believe."

"Yes, but I don't see what he has to do with you."

"There was a mix-up at the clinic."

Jenny's blue eyes darkened to amethyst and widened dramatically. "What sort of a mix-up?"

"To put it simply, they gave you my sperm."

"That's not possible," she said with a finality that made his blood boil. "I was inseminated with donor sperm—"

"And I was the donor," he interrupted angrily.

"I don't believe it," Jenny returned just as angrily. "Why would they tell you something like that and not tell me?"

"I told them not to," he replied, stunning her into silence. "I wanted the…pleasure of telling you myself."

Jenny snorted her disbelief.

"If you don't believe me, call the clinic."

"I don't know the number." Jenny turned back to the window in an obvious attempt to end the conversation.

Matt recited the number from memory. "Call them now, Miss Ames." When she hesitated, he bristled. "Do it."

Jenny picked up the receiver and quickly dialed the number. Dr. Bentley was in, as Matt knew he would be. That was one of the benefits of having a dozen blood-thirsty lawyers waiting for the order to pounce. It assured round-the-clock service from everyone.

How he wished he could hear the doctor's end of the conversation.

"Dr. Bentley?" Jenny began softly. "Yes, Mr. Hanson is here now."

Her voice dropped even lower. "He says there was a mix-up at the clinic. Why didn't you warn me about this...? Yes, I did get the message that you'd called, but I thought it was about scheduling an appointment. Don't you think you should have called me back, for heaven's sake?"

Matt imagined the doctor's explanation—if indeed there was an explanation for such blatant incompetence—and his abject apology.

"I don't care if he threatened you with a thousand lawyers..." she said finally.

"It was only twelve," Matt muttered.

"You shouldn't have given him my name. If the only connection between the two of us is a number on my chart, and his sample no longer exists, how do you know it was given to me? There were other women there that day."

Matt shifted in place, listening to Jenny's arguments but refusing to consider them. It wasn't as if he hadn't gone over this in a hundred times in his own mind. He *knew* the truth. And soon Miss Ames would, too.

"No, I don't see. It doesn't make any sense. Check your records again and you'll find you've made yet another mistake. We discussed my decision to go with an unknown donor, and I believed you understood my reasons."

"No father, no complications, Miss Ames?" he said under his breath, the muttering turning into a growl this time.

As he watched, Jenny put out a hand to steady herself against the window frame. The fingers that grazed the glass pane trembled. He stood ready to catch her if she should faint, but he doubted it would be necessary. This was one strong little woman.

Jenny closed her eyes as she listened, then shook her head slowly. "No," she said firmly. "No."

Matt wondered what the doctor was saying. He hoped it didn't have anything to do with his behavior at the clinic. He never wanted anyone to know about that. He'd gone there to correct the mistake of banking his boys in the first place, then threatened a lawsuit over the "redirection" of his precious sperm. When the doctor told him he was going to be a father, he'd fainted dead away.

"I don't have an attorney." Jenny's voice wavered, yet she spoke with a force that evidenced a steel will. "I won't need one unless you persist in giving my name and work address to strange men."

Matt resented being called strange, but said nothing. He had a feeling he knew how this conversation was going to play out, and already he didn't like it.

"As I said before, I don't accept this so-called mistake. There will be no amniocentesis, no DNA tests. She's my baby."

If the satisfied look on Jenny's face meant anything, that was that.

"You understand I won't be returning to the clinic for prenatal visits? Very good. At least you understand that much."

Jenny slammed down the receiver, then faced Matt.

Based on the red tint of her cheeks, she was obviously very angry.

"Those people are completely incompetent."

"Then you agree a mistake was made."

"I'm not a stupid woman, Mr. Hanson. If your sperm is missing, obviously something happened. I don't think we'll ever know what. I'm sorry you were involved. But this is my baby, she's healthy and that's all I care about."

"I heard you say you wouldn't have amniocentesis."

"I won't."

"Then how do you know the baby is a girl?"

"From experience. I'm the latest in the long line of female-only children. It's been so long since a boy was born into our family no one remembers what the family name is anymore."

"The father determines the sex of the child, not the mother's family background."

She closed her eyes and took one impatient breath, then another. When she opened them the look she gave him was chilling.

"If it makes you feel any better, I had an ultrasound several months ago. It wasn't the clearest image, but I'm perfectly happy with the results. Look, you need to understand something. I don't care who the father is. I certainly won't hold you responsible for any mistakes made at the clinic."

She sure was articulate when she was angry. Matt hoped he never had to sit across a bargaining table from this little wildcat. Those eyes, so soft and serene before, were flashing a warning now.

"But the baby could be a boy. My *son*."

Jenny began to shake her head again. Matt knew she was resisting the possibility she was carrying his child, and while her stubbornness irritated him, he admired it too, since, as his mother always said, stubborn was his middle name.

Oh, Lord, what a mess. He was going to have a child, possibly a son, despite what Jenny Ames said about her illustrious female antecedents, and he didn't yet have a wife. "I think we should get married."

"What?" Jenny asked, as though he were speaking a language she didn't comprehend.

"We should get married."

"I don't want to get married." She straightened her back and looked down her pert nose at him. "I don't *need* to get married. This is my life, my very own, perfectly contented life, and believe me, Matthew Robert Hanson, you are not in it."

"Why?" he persisted, ignoring the tiny flare of satisfaction in her remembering his name.

All three of his names.

"Don't tell me you're one of those women who doesn't like men."

"I like men fine, although I fail to see how that's any of your business. I simply didn't plan to involve anyone else in this pregnancy. It was my choice to be a single mother, and I stand by it."

"I will not allow my child to be born illegitimate," Matt shouted.

Jenny grew quiet, and he knew he was treading on shaky ground.

"There are worse things in the world than being illegitimate, Mr. Hanson."

"Like what?"

"Like being unwanted. Being left in the care of someone who doesn't like children. Being less important than your parents' desires."

"If you're speaking from experience, Jenny—" his voice softened "—I'm sorry."

"Apology accepted." She straightened her jacket with a sharp tug. "Now, would you please leave? I have work to do."

"How much?"

She looked up, seemingly surprised that he hadn't scampered out the door when she'd dismissed him.

"Excuse me?"

"How much do you want for the baby? We could sign a contract…consider you a surrogate mother. I'll pay for the remainder of your confinement and then settle a lump sum on you when you have the baby and turn it over to me."

"It? *It!*"

Matt saw her small hands ball into fists, her knuckles turning white as she fought to contain her anger. While he admired her spirit, he was more than a little annoyed by her obvious lack of regard for his rights as a father. Rights he took very seriously, indeed.

"My child is not for sale. What kind of woman do you think I am?"

Her voice was as sharp as the edge of a knife, the kind a less civilized woman would have used to run him through. Yet Matt couldn't resist another jibe.

"The kind of woman who gets pregnant with donor sperm and doesn't care who the father is?" The moment the words left his mouth, he regretted them.

He watched as Jenny's eyes narrowed and the rise and fall of her breaths matched the clenching and unclenching of her hands. Her voice dropped, low and deadly. "I may not know who my baby's father is, but I know her mother, and she's not a woman who suffers fools gladly. Get out."

Matt felt like an idiot. He'd built a business on reading people; their intentions, their hopes and dreams, their vulnerabilities. And now he'd reduced Jenny Ames to a dollar sign without knowing her at all.

He paused before he spoke again, wondering if there was a way to take back all the impulsive things he'd done and said since he'd walked into her office. Marking it all up to his surprise at the news of his impending fatherhood simply didn't cut it.

"Miss Ames. Jenny," he said, walking toward her slowly. He stopped when there was but a step between them to gauge whether or not it was safe to speak to her this close up.

When she didn't run or scream or slap him for being such a jackass, he reached out and took her hand.

In what he hoped was a soothing gesture, he rubbed the pad of his thumb across the pale, silky skin of her hand. She flinched, but he didn't think she was repelled by his touch.

It was his own reaction that surprised him even more. With her hand in his he felt a connection, a jolt of something unexpected. Did she feel the surge of electricity that shot through him and nearly made his heart stop beating?

"I'm sorry," he said, forcing a tone of conviction into his voice. "That was stupid. I've offended you when I really only meant to express my very real concern for the child. I hope you will allow me to make amends. I have resources that can be put at your disposal if you have needs you can't meet on your own."

"The only thing I want from you is your absence." She thrust home her point by jerking her hand from his.

"You're throwing me out?"

"You're quick," she said lightly, but with a hint of sarcasm. "One thing before you leave, though. Somewhere, *out there,* is a woman who'd be overjoyed to marry you and have your children. Go, Mr. Hanson. Go find her. *Leave me alone.*"

"I still believe that baby you're carrying is mine."

"Believe what you like. It doesn't change a thing."

"You're wrong," Matt countered, believing it with his whole soul. "It changes everything, for all three of us."

With one last look, Matt turned and walked to the door. The battle might be lost, but the war was most definitely still up for grabs.

Chapter Two

"What did Matt Hanson want with you?"

Jenny struggled to lift her gaze to meet Nancy's. She did so in time to see her assistant in total panic.

"Jenny? Are you all right? My God, you're as white as a sheet."

Nancy rushed into the conference room and knelt in front of Jenny's chair.

"You're shivering. Take my jacket."

Jenny has happy to have the extra covering. Matt Hanson's unexpected visit had frightened her, shaken her and stolen every last bit of warmth from her body.

"I wish you'd say something," Nancy implored. "You're scaring me to death."

"I'm all right," Jenny managed through quivering lips. "A little stunned, I guess."

"What did Matt want?"

"You know him?"

Nancy nodded. "We grew up in the same neighborhood."

Jenny had forgotten the reason she'd hired Nancy Patterson as her assistant. Mostly she'd planned to mine the perky brunette's contacts for supporters for the foundation's many programs to help women and children, but instead they'd become friends. Today Jenny hoped her friend could help her make sense out of what appeared to be a monumental mess.

"Who is he? When he said his name I thought it sounded familiar, but right now I can't get my brain wrapped around it. He said we'd never met."

"I'm surprised. He's Hanson Associates…you know, the company that owns practically all of downtown."

"Why would anyone want to own downtown? It's doing fine by itself."

"Because that's what multimillionaires do."

"Multi?"

"Megamulti. They say there's never been anything Matt Hanson wanted that he didn't get."

Jenny felt the blood draining from her head. She covered her face with her hands. "This is going to be bad. Really bad."

"Why? What did he want?"

"My baby," Jenny said quietly.

"Your what?"

She looked up and smiled ruefully as she realized Nancy shared her own stunned look. "He says Alexis is his."

Nancy sat down abruptly. She opened her mouth to speak, then closed it just as quickly. When she caught Jenny's gaze she asked, "Is she?"

"No," Jenny said quickly, then paused, remembering Matt's conviction. "I don't know. The doctor who did the insemination says yes. Matt Hanson firmly believes it."

"What are you going to do?"

"Nothing."

"What do you mean, nothing? You can't dismiss a man like Matt Hanson."

"Watch me."

"Jenny, this isn't wise. Somebody told this guy he's going to be a father. I don't think you can underestimate a thing like that."

Jenny sighed. "You're probably right. I'll speak with an attorney," she said reluctantly.

Nancy looked skeptical.

"I will," she insisted. "I promise."

Jenny rose and went to the room's tiny kitchenette. She poured a glass of water, then drank it slowly.

"Nancy, why would a megamultimillionaire make a deposit at a sperm bank?"

"You really cut to the chase, don't you? It's just gossip. Fresh gossip, I'll admit, but Matt was engaged to Krystal McDonnough for over a year."

"The model?"

"The very one, but they broke up about a month ago. Rumor says the reason for the split was that Krystal decided she didn't want children." Nancy, uncharacteristically nervous, wrung her hands. "God, I can't believe I'm talking about this. I've never repeated anything so personal about anyone in my life."

"Tell me!"

"I will, but I need to start with a disclaimer. Matt Hanson is an intensely private person, Jenny. If he knew that you were privy to his personal business, I think he'd be upset."

"I can't see that his love of privacy stopped him from prying into my medical history and coming after me," Jenny said angrily.

"I guess you have a point. Tit for tat, huh?" She laid her hands on the table and sighed, obviously reluctant to reveal what she knew. Jenny's curiosity overshadowed her compassion for Nancy's place on the hot seat.

"Krystal's best friend is a slimeball named Cherie. She gets her hair done at the same salon as my sister."

"This isn't going to be one of those urban legends where your mother's brother's sister-in-law's cousin's mechanic saw a UFO, is it?"

"Do you want to hear this or not?"

"Go ahead." Jenny sat down and fiddled with a pencil, fully prepared to take copious notes.

"Cherie said Krystal tricked Matt into the engagement by telling him she wanted to have a family. Then after she got the ring—seven carats, flawless—she pretended to be afraid of getting pregnant because it would hurt her career. They decided to postpone the babies. Matt went to the family planning clinic and Krystal was going to bank her eggs, just in case they waited too long. Then they broke up. I guess the rest is history."

Jenny's mind whirled. It didn't take a math whiz to put one and one together and get three. Matt Hanson's sperm and Jenny Ames's egg equaled one sweet little baby girl.

She planted her hands on the tabletop and rose. "No."

"No?"

"There was no mistake. Alexis is not Matt Hanson's baby."

"I wouldn't dismiss him so easily if I were you. He's got a reputation around town as a ruthless businessman. If he thinks that baby is his, he could make a lot of trouble for you."

"What could he do? Take my baby? I don't think so. In this case, possession is one hundred percent of the law."

Nancy shook her head. "I don't know, Jenny. I remember when Matt's father died. He was only eleven or twelve at the time. He was devastated. Knowing what it was like for him to grow up without a father, I don't imagine it's a state he'd wish on his own child."

"This *is not* his child."

"How are you going to prove that?"

"I don't have to prove anything. I'm going to deal with it by completely ignoring him."

"Do you think that's going to work? The look on his face when he left here wasn't the look of a man who'll go down without a fight."

Jenny thought of her own father, whom she hadn't seen for years. "He'll get over it," she said bitterly. "They always do."

Fuming, Matt returned to the office where he bought struggling companies, turned them around, then sold them for a profit—where no one ever told him no.

It took him an hour to get his emotions under control, then he summoned Greg McBride, the head of his legal team, and described his meeting with the very independent Ms. Ames.

For once the Daniel Webster of the courtroom was speechless.

"You met her without a lawyer present? What were you thinking?"

"Don't worry. Nothing happened." Remembering the look on Jenny's face when he'd left her made him amend his comment.

"Nothing much, anyway. The woman in question doesn't want to have anything to do with me."

"But you're the baby's father!"

"Tell *her* that. Maybe then she'd get the message that I'm not going to let my son grow up without a father."

"Didn't Ms. Ames say the baby is a girl?"

"She said she had a fuzzy ultrasound picture. That's not enough evidence for me. It could be a boy."

"Does that mean you're not interested unless the baby's male?"

"Don't be ridiculous." It seemed as though everyone was on his case today, and he was getting tired of it. "You of all people should know me better than that."

Matt stood and walked to the window, surveying the breathtaking view of multicolored fall leaves and the fast-flowing Ohio River. It was on days like today he wanted to get on his boat and make a run for it. He grew pensive, remembering childhood as a lonely, melancholy time without his dad. "It's a sign."

Greg exploded with laughter. "Since when do you believe in signs?"

"Since the Cole deal fell through."

"Cole? The man whose building burned down?"

"The very same. On the day he came in to close the deal I noticed a small, round burn on his tie. It was probably from a cigarette; he smoked like a chimney. Anyway, I had a bad feeling about it. When he began to press for concessions, I backed out. He left, and three days later his factory was destroyed. If I'd put my name on that contract, it would have been my building."

"You think he torched the place?"

"No, the fire marshal ruled it accidental. But still—"

"A sign."

"Definitely a sign."

"And Jenny Ames?"

"Most definitely a sign. I couldn't be more convinced that baby's mine if I had been present at the conception and not just down the hall. There's no way she's going to force me out of the picture."

"How are you going to keep her from it?"

"Strategy, my friend. First, I want to know everything there is to know about Miss Genevieve Marie Ames."

"Define *everything*."

"I want to know who she is and who she's been with. I want to know who her parents are, or were. I want to know how she came to be the executive director of a foundation I've never heard of and how she's escaped my notice for so long. And I want to know why a beautiful girl like that would use artificial insemination to get pregnant and not wait for a husband to do the honors."

"That pretty, huh?"

"Prettier. She's delicate, Greg, but with a core of steel. Brave, feisty…and when she laid her hand on her belly while we were arguing I saw a maternal, protective instinct so strong it humbled me. Scared me a little bit, too. She has a glow about her I've never seen in any other woman."

"Even Krystal?"

"Especially Krystal. Krystal is kibble next to Jenny."

"You're attracted to this girl, aren't you?"

"Attracted, intrigued, totally confused. I'm still sorting it all out."

"I can't wait to meet her. In the meantime—"

"One other thing," Matt said, interrupting. "I want you to set up a trust fund for the baby. Make her the administrator."

"Slow down, buddy. You just met the girl. We don't even have conclusive proof you're the baby's father. How do you know she and that bozo at the clinic aren't running some kind of scam? Has she said anything to you about money?"

"Only that I could take it and shove it up my—" He laughed roughly. "Heck, for all I know she's having *me* investigated."

"I'll look into that, too," Greg said, his tone ominous.

"Whatever you do, make it fast," Matt ordered. "In the meantime, I'm her new best friend. She's not going to make a move unless I know about it first. The sooner I know where I stand legally, the better I'll like it."

And the sooner Jenny Ames was his, lock, stock and baby, the better he'd like that, too.

"Take the flowers, lady. Please?"

The fresh-faced deliveryman tucked his clipboard under his arm and thrust his hands into his pockets. It was a sign, Jenny supposed, that he was tired of arguing.

She knew the feeling.

If Jenny thought throwing Matt Hanson out of her office was the end of things, she'd been sadly mistaken. It had been flowers and phone calls every single day for two weeks. It was as if she was his new hobby.

The courier who'd delivered the first bouquet looked around the office with undisguised disdain, as though he'd thought the place could use some cheering up. After depositing a vase of rusty-hued Gerber daisies, he'd left.

Jenny considered writing a brief, painfully correct

thank-you note, but as the hours passed she became less and less sure of exactly what to say. She knew *buzz off* was totally inappropriate; at least her grandmother had taught her that much. When Matt called later in the day to ask how she liked the flowers, she was trapped.

Apparently encouraged, he sent more flowers the next day, and the next and the next. Jenny grew more and more frustrated. When begging him to stop didn't work, she began ignoring him, immersing herself in work.

This morning, nearly a week later, she'd barely gotten the door unlocked when the florist deliveryman showed up again.

"But I don't want them," she persisted. "The place already looks like a funeral parlor. The ones I'm taking home are dying from lack of care."

"I'm just doing my job, ma'am. If you don't want them, tell the sender."

"He won't listen! He's even more stubborn than you are!"

"Then I guess I'll see you tomorrow. Have a good day, ladies."

And with a tip of his cap to both Jenny and her assistant, he was gone.

"Arrgh!" Jenny feigned tearing out her hair.

"Maybe you're not going about this correctly," Nancy said with a grin. "I've heard you on the phone. " 'The flowers are lovely, but…' 'The colors are heavenly, but…' Then you wimp out. If you don't want any more flowers, say so. Tell him you're allergic. Tell him they make you sick. Use your imagination. I've seen you get money for sick babies out of the most hardhearted donors without even breaking a sweat. All you have to do is work it, girlfriend."

Jenny struck her most vampish pose and tossed back her shoulder-length hair, then spoiled the effect by waddling toward the phone. She dialed Matt's number from memory, ignoring Nancy's smirk. She'd called his office enough times to beg him to stop the deliveries. How could she not know his number?

"Jenny," he said when he came on the line. "Is everything all right?"

How nice of him to step so readily into her trap. Jenny smiled at Nancy and batted her eyelashes.

"Well, Mr. Hanson, since you asked…it's about the flowers." Jenny added a little tremor to her voice and Nancy gave her a thumbs-up.

"Call me Matt," he said quickly. "What's wrong with the flowers?"

"Well," Jenny began slowly, sounding as innocent as she could. "They're beautiful, really…"

Nancy began to frown, and Jenny waved her off.

"But there are so many of them that the smell is beginning to bother me. I feel…nauseated. You know, morning sickness, only all day long."

"Oh, that's too bad. I thought you liked them. That's what you said the last time we talked."

Uh, oh. Busted. Jenny began to sweat.

"They're lovely, honest. I took some home to my neighbors, and the people on the bus said you must be the most thoughtful man in the world."

From the silence on the line, Jenny thought they'd been disconnected.

"What bus?" He sounded as though he was choking on the words.

"Excuse me?"

"You said the people on the bus. What bus?"

"The Metro?" Didn't he know anything? She couldn't believe she was explaining herself like this. "The one I take to and from work every day?"

"Don't you know how to drive?"

"Of course I know how to drive. I just don't own a car."

"How can you not own a car in a city the size of Cincinnati? How do you get around?"

"I take the bus. Or I walk. If I need to, I can call a cab or hire a car. But really, this is an easy place to get around on foot."

"Oh, no, don't tell me. You've climbed the steps," he said, referring to the extensive network of stone stairs that criss-crossed the city.

"Yep," she admitted. "More than once, and I've got the T-shirts to prove it."

His voice turned skeptical. "But not lately," he said slowly.

"Yes, lately, Matt."

There was a pause, then a hearty *gotcha* kind of a laugh.

"Do you realize you called me Matt? That's an accomplishment that deserves a reward."

"That's not necessary, Mr., uh, Matt. Don't you understand? I don't want anything from you."

Jenny looked frantically at Nancy. *Help,* she mouthed.

Don't look at me, Nancy mouthed back.

"I'm sending a driver over, Jenny. His name is John Steadman, and don't you dare send him back. There will be a car at your disposal for as long as you need it. I don't want to hear about you even looking at a bus again."

"Matt, I don't need a car and driver. I can ride the bus. I've been riding it all my life. This is my city. It's what I do."

"Not anymore," he said firmly.

"Okay," Jenny murmured, defeated, into the now-silent receiver. She hung up the phone and glared at her very unhelpful assistant.

"What happened?" she asked. "I was in control. I was. Had him eating right out of the palm of my hand." She held up an empty hand as proof. "Then, boom! He gave me a chauffeur. We were talking about flowers, victory was within my grasp, and suddenly I've got a chauffeur."

"He's good," Nancy finally conceded. "I've known guys who were good, but Matt Hanson, he's *GOOD!*"

Chapter Three

The following morning a knock at the door interrupted Jenny's routine. A peek through sheer lace curtains revealed Matt Hanson on her porch.

"Good morning, Jenny," he called through the door, irritating her with the merry lilt of his voice. "Mr. Steadman and I are here to take you to work."

"Thanks," she shouted back. "But not necessary. I'm running a little late this morning. Go ahead without me." She turned away from the door and then, as an afterthought, repeated, "Thanks."

"Open up, Jenny."

She flung the door open angrily. "Or what?" she asked pointedly. "You'll huff and you'll puff and you'll blow my house down?"

"Something like that," he answered, his voice calm and steady.

"Do you ever take no for an answer? I've asked you to leave me alone. Now I must insist. *Go away.*"

"Are you always this cranky in the morning?"

"I'm not cranky. I'm plain, dog tired. Lexie's practiced her gymnastics routine for eight hours straight and I'm bruised from the inside out. I don't think I slept more than ten minutes at a time the entire night."

"Lexie?" he said slowly.

"Uh, yeah. Short for Alexis."

"You've already picked out a name?" He actually sounded hurt.

"I really do not need this," she muttered.

"Lexie?" he said, again, and this time he made a face.

"Single mother's prerogative," she snapped, grabbing her coat from the bentwood rack by the door and slipping her arms into the sleeves. She buttoned the top button, the only one that fit, while Matt looked on in horror.

"That's your coat?" he shouted. "It doesn't even meet in the front."

It was too much. Tears that had been threatening all morning poured down her cheeks. It was more than she could bear.

"What do you want from me?" she sobbed. "You don't like my baby's name. My coat's not good enough."

Matt drew a handkerchief from his pocket and stepped forward to blot her cheeks. She took a swift step back.

"Don't touch me," she said, sounding a little like the possessed girl from The Exorcist.

"I didn't mean to criticize, Jenny. Alexis is a beautiful name…for a girl…and your coat is, ah, very nice. I was only worried that you might get cold."

Jenny could tell he wanted to ask if this was the coat she'd worn to wait for the bus.

"It will fit fine after the baby's born. It seemed frivolous to buy another one when I won't be able to wear it again." She snatched the handkerchief from his hand and dried her face.

. "Jenny," he said softly.

"Shut up, okay? Just shut up."

She could tell he was about to answer, but he nodded instead.

"If you expect me to ride to work with you, you'd better not say another word."

"Okay," he said, then froze when she nailed him with a frown.

"And you'd better not send me any more flowers, either," she added for good measure.

"No more flowers, I swear. Never another flower."

When Matt arrived to collect Jenny for the trip home, the first thing he noticed was the lack of color in her cheeks, and her red-rimmed eyes. He said nothing, merely held up her coat so that she could slip her arms into the sleeves, then walked her to the car.

She greeted Steadman, but resisted any attempt at conversation. She refused the offer of something to drink. He pulled a blanket from the storage next to the seat and covered her from chest to feet. Jenny didn't protest.

As the car pulled out into traffic, Matt heard a deep sigh from Jenny's side of the broad bench seat. It was followed by a muffled sob. He slipped his handkerchief from his pocket, made a mental note to ask his housekeeper to buy a dozen more and handed it over without looking.

"I apologize for my behavior this morning. You had every right to call me cranky."

"I probably shouldn't have sprung myself on you the way I did. I only wanted to help." As an apology it stank, but it was the best he could do, considering how long it had been since he'd apologized for anything. He decided not to mention the argument about her coat or the baby's name.

"I know, but I think it would be better if you'd go your way and let me go mine."

"I'll think about it," he lied smoothly, knowing there was no way he'd let her slip from his life before he knew whether or not the baby in her belly was his.

She must have thought him sincere, because he felt her relax into the plush seat. From the corner of his eye he could see her eyes were closed and that her head had fallen back, mouth slightly open, the sheen of tears still on her cheeks.

His heart clenched. How could he let this brave and gentle woman out of his life? Didn't she know how much she needed him, how much a child needed a father?

Funny, how he'd never once doubted the doctor's assertion that he was the baby's father. The first impulse of most men would be to deny paternity, but here he was welcoming it, demanding it. Somehow he knew when he held his baby he'd be the happiest man alive.

But what to do about Jenny? She didn't believe there'd been a mix-up at the clinic, or that Matt was the father of her child. There was even that silly thing about her girls-only heritage. Yet here she was in his car, accepting his help, putting up only token resistance—well, maybe a little more than token—to his presence in her life.

Jenny shifted, and the soft blanket fell away from her shoulders to rest in a puddle at her waist, or at least what was left of it. Her midsection taunted him from between the open edges of her coat. Matt cursed silently, his emotions warring between wanting to run his hands over her pregnant belly and rushing to the nearest store to buy her a new coat.

If she didn't like something as simple as flowers, she most likely wouldn't appreciate mink or sable. Maybe he could leave his cashmere Burberry at her house, accidentally, of course, although that might be a problem if she continued to refuse—as she had that morning— to let him step through her door.

Well, he wasn't the scourge of Cincinnati's business district for nothing. He'd work it out. He'd get his way eventually.

Jenny turned, mumbled something unintelligible, then began sliding toward him with alarming speed. He barely got his arms around her before she thudded to a stop against his chest. He was glad for the softness of his coat, if only because it would cushion her as she rested. Jenny mumbled again, and snuggled closer, all her feisty resistance gone.

The fresh scent of her drifted up to tease and tantalize his nostrils. No heavy, provocative perfumes for Jenny. She smelled as pure and natural as a spring morning on the water, and just as tempting.

He'd finally gotten the girl into his arms in the back seat of his car. He wasn't sixteen anymore, but it was pure heaven, all the same.

"Home, Mr. Hanson?" the chauffeur asked.

"Once around the park, I think." He chuckled softly. "It appears our fair lady has fallen asleep."

"Jenny?" Nancy stood at the office door looking sheepish. "I'm sorry."

"What happened?"

"Well, Matt called and asked if you were free for

lunch. I told him you had meetings today and that we'd decided to order in."

"So what's there to be sorry about?"

Nancy was quiet for a moment, then said, "He sent over a caterer and she's in the conference room."

"Tell her to go away."

"It's too late. I heard the microwave beep." Nancy's voice dropped to a conspiratorial whisper. "I think there's soup."

Jenny's mouth gaped. "Is this place bugged? How could he have known we were wishing for soup?" Actually she'd wished for chili, Cincinnati-style, but when heartburn loomed, common sense prevailed. And soup ran a close second.

"Intuition?" Nancy laughed, her brown curls bouncing. "Hey, it's cold. Soup is comfort food, and lord knows your comfort is uppermost in his mind lately."

"I wish he wouldn't—"

"Why not?" Nancy asked abruptly, disapprovingly. "Matt Hanson could take care of you in ways you can only imagine. He's got money and power and looks."

Yes, Jenny had to admit, he was rich and powerful. Everything about him made her nervous, but also incredibly curious.

Heaven help her, she was already falling into his trap. When she'd awakened in his arms last night she'd been embarrassed beyond words. Her neighbor called to ask if everything was all right and said the limo sat at the curb for nearly an hour before Matt helped Jenny out and silently escorted her to the door.

And yet, when he'd shown up that morning, all windtossed and too delicious for words, she'd put on her coat and gone with him like a lamb to the slaughter. Something in her melted at the sight of him, made her think of possibilities best left unexplored.

Stupid, stupid, stupid, she chided herself. This foolishness had to stop and it had to stop now. A man like Matt would never want her once he really knew her.

"Nancy, I can take care of myself. I thought long and hard before I made the decision to have Lexie without a husband. I know it won't be easy, but I believe it's for the best. I've met at least a hundred single mothers through my work for the foundation and I know it can be done. My grandfathers walked away physically and my own father did the same thing emotionally. I'll do everything in my power to keep my little girl from going through that."

When Lexie gave her a swift kick in the side, Jenny reflected on the difficulty of motherhood, even before birth.

"Besides," she said, hoping to take a little more of the wind out of Nancy's sails, "he's made it painfully clear that I'm not good enough. You should have seen the way he acted about my coat the other morning."

"But—"

"I don't need a man to take care of me, or use or abandon me…"

"Abandon? What on earth are you talking about?"

"Nothing. Forget it. What time is my meeting with the United Way people?

"Not for another hour. You have plenty of time to eat a good hot lunch."

"I don't want his food," she grumbled.

"Don't be silly. It's free, and the deli's not going to

be able to send up anything half this good. You'll save some money for the little kumquat's college fund and get your vitamins at the same time."

Her secretary paused at the door, then turned. "Jenny, I know I work for you, but I consider myself your friend, too."

"Oh, Nancy. Of course you're my friend."

"Matt's not a monster." Noting Jenny's frown, she continued. "Well, he is a little pushy. Okay, a lot pushy, but if what he says is true—"

Jenny opened her mouth to protest, but Nancy waved her comments off as if she were swatting flies.

"If what he says is true, he has every right to try to help you any way he can. If you ask me, that's a pretty noble thing. That baby deserves the best you can give her now, not only after she's born."

Defeated, Jenny sat back and hugged her belly. "Nancy, I know I've been difficult, but believe me, I have my reasons." And being abandoned was just the beginning.

"You've not been difficult at all," Nancy countered, blissfully unaware of Jenny's inner turmoil. "You're entitled to whatever feelings you have by virtue of being pregnant. I just don't think you should let this *stuff* get in the way of the USDA's nutritional guidelines." She giggled merrily. "Now, unless you want us to get thrown in the slammer for violation of the food pyramid, we'd better eat. Would you like me to bring your lunch to you here, or will you join me in the conference room?"

Jenny stood, laughing through her apprehensions. "The conference room sounds fine. Besides, I'd like to thank the caterer."

"Excellent idea." Nancy grinned, angling her elbow outward like a tuxedoed escort. "What do you say we do lunch?"

Jenny wondered for the umpteenth time what John Steadman thought of his new assignment as her chauffeur.

When he dropped by the office one frigid afternoon a week after the caterer first showed up, she also wondered if he was spying for Matt Hanson.

It would have been simple. There were no secrets in the small office, no stealth, no subterfuge.

And if he thought there was, Jenny was going to take care of that in short order.

"Mr. Steadman, there's a problem at one of the children's homes we fund downtown. One of the babies has a fever and needs to go to the doctor. The taxi service that usually helps us out is unavailable. Will you drive the center's director and the child to the doctor's office? It's an emergency."

To her surprise, he jumped to his feet and grabbed his hat.

"A baby, you say? Poor little tyke. If you'll give me the address, I'll leave right away."

Jenny's thank-you hung in the air. He was gone before the words were out of her mouth.

Nancy's voice came at her out of the quiet.

"What on earth were you thinking? When Hanson finds out about this, he'll throw a fit."

Jenny turned with a look of wide-eyed innocence on her face. "Do you think so? Really?"

"You did that on purpose." Nancy pressed her lips together in a mock frown, then smiled. "Of course you did. Since when does the taxi service turn us down?"

Jenny returned her assistant's smile. "And when Mr. Hanson finds out about it, he'll pull his chauffeur-secret-agent out of here so fast it will make our heads spin. Then with any luck he'll decide I'm too much bother and we can get back to normal."

"Normal? I think it'll be a little dull," Nancy said morosely.

"I like dull." A wistfulness softened Jenny's voice. "Besides, he was bound to lose interest sooner or later. He's no different from any other man I've ever known. When they find something they want they go great guns to get it. Then when it doesn't drop into their laps within two minutes flat, they get bored and go on to the next challenge."

"Somehow I don't think Matt's like that," Nancy said uncertainly.

"I don't really care." Jenny turned and headed toward her office, trying to walk away from her fear of the unknown. "I just want to live a nice, quiet life, help people and have my baby. A nice full, dull life."

"Well," Nancy mused. "You can try it, but if you ask me, nothing around here is ever going to be the same again."

Jenny sat in her office the rest of the afternoon and waited for all hell to break loose.

It didn't.

She expected Matt Hanson to come storming into the room demanding to know who she thought she was, using his chauffeur like a…heck, a chauffeur.

She had her answer ready. *If you don't like it, Mr. Hanson, you can…* She would insert the proper sentiment later, depending on how angry Mr. Hanson was and how angry he made her.

Then he would go away, she could breathe a sigh of relief and get on with her life.

But if that was such a good thing, why did the idea bother her so much?

Chapter Four

"Hard day?"

Jenny turned to see Matt standing at her office door, looking good enough to eat, if she did say so. Not that he looked any different now than he had when he and Mr. Steadman picked her up that morning. He'd looked pretty darn spectacular then, too, in his camel jacket and conservative tie. The Burberry coat slung across his shoulder gave him a hint of don't-give-a-damn confidence.

His eyes scanned the room, seeming to take in everything. He frowned when his gaze rested on her chair, an old cracked-leather piece of junk that made her back hurt. His attention returned to her and he stared. *At her hair.* Her hair? She realized he hadn't seen it down until today. She reached up, nervously fingering the blunt-cut ends.

It was bizarre, being eyed this way, subjected to such

intense scrutiny. Her periwinkle-blue dress was his next victim. He missed nothing…the woven ties that let out the fullness of the skirt, the buttons that decorated the bodice, the slender gold chain around her neck. His eyes met hers, and he smiled. She wondered if he suspected she favored the dress because it brought out the color of her eyes. It was her only vanity, the wearing of blue.

"Ready to go?" he asked. "I thought we might stop somewhere for dinner, or we could get some take-out, if you'd prefer."

"I don't think so. I still have a lot to do. I haven't made very good progress today."

"You're not still tired, are you?"

"No, I've been…distracted by other, um, issues."

"Issues?"

"*Personal* issues."

"Like what?"

"Like trying to get certain well-meaning but mis-guided persons out of my life."

"Oh. Well. That was vaguely to the point. I assume you're talking about me."

Her eyes met his, then she quickly glanced away. "Yes."

"I appreciate your recognizing the 'well-meaning' part of the equation, but I'm not so sure the 'misguid-ed' part is appropriate. If you'd have the amnio—"

"No. I won't have a test that might endanger my baby just to satisfy your curiosity."

"Is that what you think this is?" he asked softly. "Curiosity?"

She turned back toward the window, reaching around to rub her back. "Matt, please…"

"Why are you so determined to go it alone?"

"I'm only doing what I know is right for me."

"But wouldn't it be nice on occasion to have someone to lean on, a backup you could count on?" He sounded as if he thought that was possible.

"Sure, if I thought I'd ever find someone like that. In my experience, they're few and far between, especially—please forgive me—masculine someones."

"Why do I get the idea you're taking out your general disappointment in the male of the species on me?"

Jenny frowned. "I'm just saying."

"Well, I think you're wrong to lump me in with all the other guys who've let you down."

"You make it sound like a legion."

"It wasn't? Granted we've known each other for a short time, but I don't think you've found one redeeming quality in me, have you? Isn't there anything you like about me?"

"Not that I've noticed." It wasn't likely he'd fall for her feigned indifference, but she gave it a try anyway.

Sometimes self-protection could be a clumsy, inexact science.

"Well, I've noticed a thing or two about you."

"Really?"

"You're beautiful, Jenny, and intelligent, and compassionate, too, except for your prejudice against men."

Jenny's mouth dropped in surprise. She'd never thought of herself as prejudiced against men, even though, upon reflection, she realized he was right. Maybe it was a genetic thing, passed down through a long line of skeptical women.

"I'm sorry. I didn't mean to judge you unfairly. It's a habit, and obviously not a very endearing one. Truce?"

"Truce," he agreed. "Now, come over here and let me rub your back."

"What?"

"When I came in you were standing by the window rubbing it."

"Oh, it's nothing. Sometimes when I sit too long—"

"Let me rub it for you. It'll make you feel better."

"You don't have to," she said a little too quickly. "It's fine now."

Matt *tsk*ed disapprovingly and held out his hand. "Come over here. Don't be afraid of me. I won't bite."

Don't be afraid of me, little sheila. Old Alfie don't bite.

The sudden memory slammed into Jenny as the events of the worst day of her life came back in a blinding rush…the hot, slimy hands, the feeling of being trapped. *Your da said you were a looker, but I thought it was just fatherly pride talking. Come 'ere. I'll be easy with you….*

Jenny had run away screaming, that steamy, long-ago day in Australia, but she was determined not to run this time. To retreat was to show weakness. The possibility that Matt might use that weakness against her, in court or otherwise, made her square her shoulders, look him in the eye and pray he wouldn't know she was acting the most difficult role of her life.

Well, she'd show him. If he tried anything funny she could lay him low with a swift kick to the—well, she could lay him low, all right.

"I'm not afraid of you," she said with a false bravery. "But I certainly don't think it would be very professional of me to let an almost perfect stranger rub my back when I'm supposed to be working."

"I appreciate you calling me perfect, but we both know we're not strangers. Just because we don't know each other in the biblical sense doesn't mean we don't *know* each other, Jenny."

"I don't understand."

"You will." He held out his arms. "Come on."

This was such a bad idea she couldn't believe she was considering it. It had been so long since a man, any man, friend or foe, had touched her that she could barely remember it.

Against her will, or perhaps because she was so determined to show he didn't intimidate her, she approached him.

Unfortunately, she knew she didn't appear as confident as she would have liked.

She stopped a few feet from him and glanced from his chest to her belly. "This won't work. You'll never get your arms around me."

"Who said I was going to put my arms around you?"

"Oh." The word escaped in a little breath of disappointment before she could catch it.

He tried to hide his grin but failed. She appreciated the effort. Sort of.

"Closer. Let me show you how it's done."

Jenny stepped into the circle of his arms, only to have him turn her so that her shoulder nestled into the curve of his arm. Being so close to him was disconcerting and a little frightening. For a moment she lost her balance. Matt quickly lifted her hand and rested it on his chest, anchoring her to him.

Why me? she wondered. Why did he have to be so nice and yet so scary?

Jenny reminded herself, however unfairly, that he was just a man, a man like all the others she'd known. Quick to take up a challenge, either real or perceived, all were equally as quick to turn and scramble for shore when interpersonal seas got rocky. Sometimes you got to see real emotion in them, but more frequently they left a vapor trail of testosterone on their way out the door.

Matt's hand drifted up and down her back, soothing the troubles of the day. She couldn't remember when, or even if, anyone had ever held her this way. Growing up with disapproving caregivers had taught her not to seek physical contact, but she'd never stopped craving it. Being in Matt Hanson's arms was pleasant, but she knew better than to enjoy it; knew better than to want or need it, because to admit that was to concede she really couldn't do everything for herself.

Shaken, she tried to pull away. Matt drew her back into his arms with softly murmured words as he continued to soothe her aching back.

Jenny's mind began to wander to thoughts of the baby and how happy she would be after her little girl was born. She imagined the baby smiles, the powdery sweet smell of baby skin after a bath, the lullabies she'd sing. Her body, at first stiff and unresponsive, began to melt to the rhythm of Matt's touch. Through the fabric of his shirt she could feel the cadence of his beating heart. Her head dropped to his shoulder and she released the sigh she'd been holding, reluctantly accepting the comfort and tenderness he offered.

"Jenny."

The way he whispered her name nearly brought tears to her eyes. No one else had ever said it quite that way. It was as if he knew everything about her all the way down to her most minute cell; as though he called to her from across a great distance with that one softly spoken word; as if she had been lost a long, long time and he was home.

Before Jenny could say his name, before she could

call out to him in the same way, his mouth lowered to hover over hers. At first he only brushed his lips against hers. Then he seemed to change his mind and pressed his mouth against hers with purpose and more than a little passion.

She was shocked at her own eager response to the touch of his lips. She didn't want to kiss him, but she didn't want to fight him, either. Her heart did a flip-flop when his tongue traced her lips, then slipped inside to taste her more deeply.

She gasped with pleasure; he grinned in response. That small movement of his mouth, coupled with the downward stroking of his hand from the small of her back to the curve of her bottom sent a shiver of anticipation through her. She'd never experienced anything like this. She'd first tried kissing with a neighborhood boy when she was a teenager, but his efforts were sloppy and his embrace too confining. Those memories were nothing compared to this. She tucked those experiences far back into her brain's history file, determined to replace those memories with new ones of Matt.

She leaned into him, her body begging his for solace and protection. It wouldn't last, she knew, but she could have this moment.

A sharp knock at the door drove them apart. Nancy stuck her head in and smiled at them.

"If you don't need me for anything else, I'll be going now."

Embarrassed to be caught in a compromising position, Jenny smoothed her dress over her belly and caught up the knotted ends of the bows. Without looking at Nancy, she said good-night.

Matt had the gall to laugh and Nancy joined in.

Jenny's special moment was lost and she mourned it. Too angry for tears, she stalked to her desk and sat down with a plop, grabbed a bulging file and began to read. She heard the door close and assumed Nancy had left.

She hoped Matt had gone with her. They deserved each other.

The office was deadly quiet until Matt broke the silence by clearing his throat.

"Go home," she ordered.

"I didn't mean to laugh," he said without emotion. "It was a nervous reaction."

"It doesn't matter." She prayed Lexie couldn't hear her mother's lie. "It didn't mean anything."

"Maybe not for you, but when I kiss a pretty woman I don't want an audience."

"Really? You never kissed Krystal McDonnough in front of an audience?"

"What do you know about Krystal and me?" he asked coldly.

"Oh, it's okay for you to invade my privacy and talk to my doctors and come to my home uninvited but it's not okay for me to know about Krystal?"

"Answer the question. What do you know about Krystal and me?"

She quickly withered under his intense glare. Her bravado faded. "Only that you were engaged to her and broke up shortly before we met. Nancy told me."

"Then all you know is that *Krystal* kissed *me* in public, not the other way around. I never liked making a show of our relationship, although it seemed to be one of her favorite things."

"I don't care." She knew she sounded like a petulant child, but she didn't care about that, either.

"Fine. Then we won't have to argue about it any-more. Get your coat. We're going home."

"You go. I'll take the bus."

"Fine," he shouted.

"Fine," she shouted back as he walked out the door, slamming it behind him.

She didn't cry because of the interrupted kiss, or because they argued, or even because he'd left her alone in an empty office. She cried because the best example of her precious ability to take care of herself, of being a strong and independent woman, was the stupid city bus.

He'd been waiting in the lobby, cursing and pacing for the better part of an hour when Jenny stepped off the elevator. She appeared only momentarily surprised to see him, then her features settled into a mask of indifference.

He blocked the door as she tried to sweep past him, as regal in her disdain as any society matron in the Queen City. He reached for her and fastened the button at her throat, grumbling all the while about stubborn women and cheap winter coats.

Outside, the chauffeur stood next to the limousine, ready to open the door for his passengers.

"Get in the car. I'd rather Steadman didn't know we've been arguing."

Jenny nodded but refused to meet his gaze. Matt felt like a heel. He could see she'd been crying, probably ever since he'd left her office.

They rode in silence. The possibility of upsetting Jenny again was reason enough for Matt not to speak. That was the thing about women and their tears; they used them like a weapon, and when you got hit, you knew it.

When the car stopped and she struggled to get out,

he touched her hand. She stilled as he rubbed his fingers over the silky flesh of her wrist, imagining he could feel the quickening of her pulse.

"Have dinner with me tomorrow night," he said.

"No."

"Saturday, then."

"I can't."

"Why not?" He couldn't believe the ridiculous conversation. When had he ever begged a woman to share a meal with him? "How long are you going to make me pay for wanting to kiss you? Was it such a sin?"

"It's not that. I don't care about that silly kiss. I've forgotten the whole incident. Perhaps you should, too."

"Then if it's not the kiss, why won't you go out with me?"

"I can think of a thousand reasons, but the primary one is that the foundation is having a banquet for our charities on Saturday night and I have to be there."

"Is anyone escorting you?" If anyone was, he could easily arrange for them to wake up with a couple of broken legs on Saturday morning.

"I don't need an escort. I can get there fine on my own."

"Give it a rest, will you? What time do I pick you up?"

Jenny sighed, and pulled her hand from his. "Six o'clock. The banquet starts at seven, but I need to be there early to check the tables and decorations. I'm warning you, you'll be bored."

"I doubt that," Matt said firmly, ignoring the fire in her eyes and the way they darkened and shimmered when she was angry or miffed. He wondered what it would be like to watch her while they made love. He would put a spark in those eyes—if he ever got the chance.

Chapter Five

"I've got the investigator's report on Jenny Ames, boss."

Matt looked up from a spreadsheet to greet his attorney. "What's it say?"

"You're not going to like it."

"Then give it to me straight. My dad always said you can't deal with a thing until you see it in the light of day."

"Here goes. Bear with me on the names, okay?" Greg shifted his papers on his knee and settled in to the plush leather chair opposite Matt's antique mahogany desk.

"Genevieve Marie Ames was born here in Cincinnati. She's thirty years old, never married."

Matt nodded. That last, at least, he knew.

"Parents, Richard and Margaret Blanding Ames. They're living in Australia in some kind of artists' colony with about a dozen other wannabe writers and filmmakers. Investigator says they do a little wife swapping on the side."

"Are you serious?"

"It's right here in the report," Greg said, tapping a finger on the papers he held.

"Jeez." Matt shook his head in amazement. "What else?"

"When Jenny was five, they left her here in Cincinnati with her maternal grandmother, Abigail March Blanding. When she died unexpectedly Jenny went to live with her great-grandmother, Virginia Prescott March."

"Do you think we could dispense with the begatting and get to the point?"

"The begatting is the point, Matt. Jenny has never lived with her parents."

"You make it sound like she was handed down from caregiver to caregiver like a pair of old shoes."

"Maybe so, but it would be accurate."

Matt's shoulders, then his whole body, clenched with anger. Who the hell did these people think they were to treat Jenny this way? "When did she last see her parents?"

"That's where the story gets sketchy. She flew to Australia to visit them when she was sixteen. Two weeks later she returned to town in the company of an Australian social worker. The reason listed on the agency's documents was inappropriate contact with a minor. I can't seem to find out exactly what that means, but there was another person—a man—involved."

"Are you saying she was raped?"

"That's not really clear. They didn't use the terms rape or assault, and the report seems pretty complete. There aren't any hospital records, which is a good sign, I think, but there's a possibility she was molested. That's what *inappropriate contact* meant back then."

"Bastards." He spat out the word. "Did anybody go to jail?"

"Apparently not. The fact that they got her out of the country and made her unavailable to testify in court may have had something to do with it. Her great-grand-mother got a child-protective order that stipulated the parents couldn't see her without supervision, but that was fourteen years ago. I don't find any records that show they've returned to this country since then."

"So, grandparents dead, parents estranged, only child. That leaves her with no family."

"Right, unless you count the baby."

"What about her personal life? She said she didn't want to marry me, but surely she didn't go through with the insemination without ever having been in a relation-ship. Was she ever engaged? Did she date?"

"The newspaper search didn't reveal any engage-ments, but then, not everyone announces. The investi-gator couldn't turn up anything personal. No problems with the neighbors, name never appeared in any police reports, no lawsuits filed, nothing."

"I guess that's good," Matt grumbled. "What's the deal with this foundation? How'd she get the job there?"

"The Prescott Foundation was formed by one of her grandmothers, the great-great, if I'm not mistaken. Their first project was to plant some flowers around a lamp-post in the old Avondale neighborhood."

Matt snorted derisively.

"Well, of course," Greg added with a grin, "that was before the turn of the century. The twentieth century. Today their assets are in the millions and they're putting about seventy-five percent of the income from it back into the community in matching grant funds each year."

"How do I get a grant?"

"First, you have to be a nonprofit organization. Having seen your financial statements from last year, I'd say you don't qualify. Then you need to have been turned down by some other grant-giving agency. Most of the groups are seeking funding for projects too small to attract the attention of the big foundations. They work with shelters, libraries, neighborhood associations, churches. The foundation places a high value on volunteerism. Even the board members serve as volunteers."

"That's not so unusual. Most people on boards serve without remuneration."

"You misunderstand. Jenny's board members volunteer at the agencies they fund. Her great-grandmother wielded a trowel at the flower planting and Jenny volunteers once a week at a home of some sort." Greg handed him a yellowed newspaper clipping showing a petite woman in a long black dress holding a wooden tray of flowers. Although the picture was faded, there was something about the woman, a softness about the eyes maybe, that reminded him of Jenny.

"Quite a family tradition," Matt conceded, if a little sarcastically. Kind of like the girl-baby thing Jenny was so proud of. "Does she have any other qualifications for the job as director? Other than familial ones, I mean."

"She has a degree in social work with a minor in psychology from the University of Cincinnati."

Matt tugged at his tie to loosen it. "Oh, Lord, not a do-gooder with a checkbook."

"It appears she knows what she's doing. The foundation is quite highly regarded. A majority of the interest and gift income goes to their clients instead of to operating costs."

"Like high salaries for the director?"

"Like that."

"Does she have enough money to live on?" It drove him crazy that Jenny hadn't bought a maternity coat, but that might have been, as she suggested, a matter of practicality. He hadn't gotten a good look at the inside of her house, but he knew it was a sturdy, fairly new structure in a good neighborhood known for its large lots. He pictured a big backyard with a swing set and sandbox. And a little brown-haired boy playing nearby.

Greg named a salary. "I'm sure it doesn't leave much room for extras, but she seems to be doing okay. She bought the house outright after selling her grandmother's place on Walnut Hill, and she started a college fund for the baby about a month after she got pregnant."

"How did I get the impression this was a wealthy family?"

"Probably the Walnut Hill connection. Fact is, they were loaded. But all Jenny got was the house and the job. The money went to the foundation."

"How do you find out all this stuff?"

"I don't ask and the investigator doesn't say. He assures me it's legal, though."

Matt considered this new information. Almost against his will, he began to admire Jenny even more than before. Clearly she was an intelligent woman who had the ability to think things through before she acted. Maybe she was right when she said she didn't need anyone to take care of her. Self-sufficiency was clearly an inherited trait in the Ames-Blanding-March-what-ever family.

"Greg? What happened to the men? The grandfather and great-grandfather, I mean. Where do they fit into the picture?"

"Well, they're not available for comment. From what I can discern, they left."

"Left? Just like that?"

"Both Jenny's grandmother and great-grandmother were granted divorces on the grounds of desertion."

"Ah. The picture begins to clear." He stood and began pacing the perimeter of his office.

"She thinks I'm going to leave, doesn't she? Yesterday I accused her of lumping me in with all the other men who'd hurt her, but I had no idea how close I'd come to the truth. Even if she did marry me, she would expect history to repeat itself." His fisted hand pounded the wall. "She thinks I'm going to betray her, too."

"Isn't that what you're planning?" Greg asked.

Matt's thoughts were spinning out of control. He hated that Jenny had been hurt, whether physically or emotionally, but the other part of him, the businessman used to getting his way, wondered how all this would affect the outcome he desired.

He should have been ashamed, but he could almost feel the baby in his arms. It made him reckless, unreasonable.

"I can't make her give us a sample of the baby's blood. If she won't allow a DNA test, how will we ever know if I'm the baby's father?"

"Actually, the courts *can* compel her to allow the test. A judge's first priority is the well-being of the child. In this state, if a man steps forward and claims to be the child's father, and promises to support the child financially and in whatever other way he can, the judge has a responsibility to seek out the truth of the paternity of the child."

"What about now? Can I demand amniocentesis?"

"Probably not. Amnio is a risky, invasive procedure

that could be hazardous to the health of the mother and child. You're going to have to wait."

"I want to know *now.*"

"It won't be long till the baby's born. Why don't you take the time to get to know Jenny better? If the two of you aren't on friendly terms it will only make things harder."

"What if we can't work things out amicably? Do you think I could get custody?"

"No, I don't."

"Why not? Because I'm a man?"

"Because she's the mother, alive and well and fully capable of raising the child herself."

"But I could still try."

"You could, but you'll have to find yourself another lawyer. I won't help you take Jenny's baby away from her. It wouldn't be right."

"You don't even know her."

Greg waved the pages of the investigator's report. "No, but I know about her. It's pretty clear to me why she decided to have a baby without a man in the picture. She's had enough hard times. I'm not going to add to them."

"When did you get to be such a humanitarian?"

"I've always had a soft spot for the underdog. Besides, my daddy would kick my butt all the way from here to Toledo if I ever did anything to hurt an expectant mom."

Matt winced. "Speaking of parents…"

"You haven't told your mother yet?"

"Not until I know something concrete."

"It shouldn't be long now."

"I'm tired of waiting. Damn, I hate it when things don't go my way."

"Matt, I cannot urge you strongly enough to stop and think about what you're doing. A moment ago you seemed angry because Jenny's family betrayed her. Now you're talking about doing the very same thing."

He tented his fingers in front of him as if considering the wisdom of advising Matt on such a personal topic.

"If you go to court and force her hand with this blood test thing, if you keep pressing on the amnio test, even though I've told you it's not safe, it begins to look as though you're not thinking of anybody but yourself. She's always going to be the child's mother, regardless of who wins and who loses."

He made it sound like a sports contest with the baby as the ball. Not that Matt wasn't perfectly willing to get down in the dirt and wrestle for possession...

Greg grumbled as he gathered up his papers and prepared to take his leave.

"Greg," Matt said sharply. The look he got in response was pure challenge. "Leave the report."

"Think about what I said, boss."

"I always listen to your advice, even if I don't follow it."

"One more thing," Greg said. Matt thought he sounded a little nervous.

"Let me have it."

"It's about Krystal. She knows."

"Aw, sh—" Matt caught himself in time, but had no doubt he'd use that word and a few more choice ones once he was alone. "How'd she find out?"

"You two were together a long time. She made friends in the office. Plus, you weren't exactly discreet when this whole thing hit the fan."

"I was taken by surprise."

Greg laughed. "You always were a master of understatement. What are you going to do?"

"Hope she stays away from me and keeps her mouth shut?"

"That's a hollow hope."

"True. I guess I'll let her make the first move. I'm too busy trying to make friends with Jenny to worry about what my ex is up to. Maybe she'll go off on a photo shoot to some deserted island and decide to stay."

"Yeah," Greg said as he walked out the door. "And maybe pigs will fly."

Matt spent the remainder of the afternoon poring over the investigator's report and what it might mean in terms of his winning or losing the right to know his child—and he was positive the baby was his.

From the moment he'd met her, Jenny had had the ability to scramble his thought processes, made him throw away every carved-in-stone business practice he'd ever held sacred. He'd always been a measure-twice, cut-once kind of guy, sizing up the competition, ensuring the outcome of every deal.

What the hell was the world coming to when a guy who planned everything in advance didn't have even the vaguest idea what he was going to do next?

He'd come within a gnat's heel of having a surgery that would have prevented him from having children for all time. His friends thought he'd lost his mind when he'd given in to Krystal's pleas to bank his sperm and have a vasectomy. Truth be told, he hadn't exactly been thinking with his brain. Other processes somewhere in his Southern hemisphere had taken over those duties.

Even now, the V-word still made him cringe.

Yeah, maybe there could have been a surgery to reverse it.

Maybe not.

Then he'd found out Krystal didn't love him, didn't want to build a family with him.

Then, a miracle. Jenny Ames was pregnant with his child.

He laughed, a humorless, angry bark. "Maybe we should forget the name Alexis and call the baby Fate instead."

The fates were against her. Except for the first month of her pregnancy Jenny hadn't been bothered by morning sickness. Yet, here it was a quarter to six, Matt would arrive any minute to take her to the party, and she was in the bathroom tossing her cookies.

Yet another sign it was not going to be a good night.

She had lived for the past couple of days with a dread that Matt would not mix well with her clients. Sure, he was presentable enough, and she knew he'd never be rude, but she didn't think he'd really get next to the concept of the shelter for homeless teenage moms or the money the foundation provided to support the seniors' poetry program at the library.

Matt was a get-out-the-checkbook-and-pay-for-what-he-wanted kind of guy, not one who would ever ask for help. He probably thought charity was for the birds—or for the lazy.

No, he definitely wouldn't fit in with her clients.

Again her stomach roiled, and she leaned toward the toilet.

A sharp knock sounded at the front door.

"Not fair," she complained to the nausea god. "Not fair at all."

"You look pale," Matt said the moment she opened the door.

"I'm all right," she protested. "Just a little evening sickness."

"Does this happen often?"

Only when I know you're coming over.

She didn't want to admit that in addition to the nausea she also got a fluttering heartbeat and a yearning in the pit of her stomach every time he arrived on the scene.

What girl wouldn't?

She'd seen handsome men before, charming ones, generous ones…but none of them had such an overwhelming personal power. And dressed as he was tonight, in an obviously custom-tailored tuxedo, his sandy hair tousled by the cool autumn wind, all he really had to do was look at her with those scrumptious chocolate-brown eyes, as he was now, and she was lost. The whole world began to melt away, and she began to fall head over heels in—

"Are you all right?"

"Huh?" Her eyes blinked—she felt the movement— and she began to breathe again, but the moment was spoiled. She had no desire to return to reality just yet, not to the man who wanted to take her child away from her.

"You were standing there staring at me, and your face flamed red, then you went white as a sheet. I thought you were going to faint. Let me in. You should lie down for a minute."

"No." She wouldn't let him into her house, her sanctuary. Not when he'd invaded every other corner of her life. "I'm fine. We'd better go or we'll be late."

"To hell with the party." He reached forward and slipped his hands under her elbows. "You're not going anywhere until I'm sure you're not going to conk out on me. When did you last eat?"

Jenny pulled away, nearly stumbling in her haste. His touch, fleeting as it was, burned a path along her skin.

"As if you didn't know. Your caterer was at the office all this week fixing lunches for everybody who walked through the door. Then she came here this morning, like some kind of meals on wheels for expectant moms."

"Are you saying you don't like her food?"

"If I do, will you make her go away?"

"Of course. But I'll keep sending someone new every day until we find a style you like."

Jenny laughed in spite of herself. "You're impossible."

"And you're not so pale anymore. I don't like it when I can't see the fire in you. Ready to go?"

"Let me get my coat."

He grabbed her hand. "Wait a minute."

Jenny frowned. Hadn't they been through this thing with her coat already?

"I have something for you. Hang on to your temper until you know what it is."

Apparently she wasn't as good at hiding her emotions as she thought.

Matt took a step back to collect a long, slender box he'd stashed on the porch. It was bound with a huge wine-colored bow. It was the kind of box that contained long-stemmed roses, dozens of long-stemmed roses, the kind of box a lover gave to his beloved on Valentine's Day.

Her arms reached for the box even before her head decided to accept the gift.

He held the box while she removed the bow with shaky hands. She lifted the lid and found not roses, but a swath of ivory colored fabric, soft and fluffy as a bunny's tail.

She looked at Matt, confused, no, mystified as to the contents of the box.

"You said no more flowers."

"And you listened," she said with a sniff, uncertain if she was disappointed or not.

"You don't like it?"

"I'm sorry, Matt." She hated feeling so ignorant and gauche, hated being reminded he was so far out of her league. "I don't know what it is."

"Allow me," he said, placing the box in her arms. He reached in and took out the fabric. When he finally held it in front of her she could see it was a cape. The softest, most beautiful—and probably the most expensive—cape she'd ever seen, long and full enough to cover and warm her and the baby.

He cares about you, a little voice inside her said. Don't spoil it by fussing about the gift.

"Thank you, Matt. It's beautiful."

He gave her a smile that made her heart leap. It was a smile that could make a less-determined woman lose her head.

Matt draped the cape around her shoulders and arranged the full collar at her throat.

"You're beautiful," he murmured as he lowered his mouth to hers. His lips were firm and warm. He used his tongue to tease open her mouth, then nibbled on her lip until she gave in to his expertise.

This was a different kiss from the one in her office, and there was no one here to disturb them. If her shivers and sighs betrayed her inexperience, she didn't care. She would have been content to stand there in the open doorway and kiss him forever if it weren't for the party.

He must have remembered, too, because he pulled back, dazzling her further with a smile.

"Very beautiful," he purred. "And now you'll be warm, too."

Jenny rolled her eyes heavenward. Score another one for Matt.

Chapter Six

"So, you're the one."

Jenny looked up as the beautiful woman bore down on her. Thanks to Nancy's show and tell she knew this was the famous—or perhaps in Matt's eyes, the infamous—Krystal McDonnough. She'd surprised everyone by showing up with one of the foundation's board members, a man who just happened to be a friend of Matt's.

"I beg your pardon?"

"The little mother. Matthew's little oops."

"Do I know you?"

"Don't be coy with me, darling. You know who I am, and I know exactly who, and what, you are."

"And exactly what am I?"

"A clever opportunist, a master schemer."

Not unlike yourself. Jenny squelched the thought. This banquet for the foundation was neither the time nor the place to indulge in the catfight the great Krystal McDonnough obviously wanted.

"What I can't figure out is how you got that doctor to do it?"

"Do what, Miss McDonnough?"

Krystal aimed a disgusted look at Jenny's belly. "That."

"It's a baby, Miss McDonnough, not a blood-sucking mutant from outer space."

"It's Matthew Hanson's baby."

"There's no proof of that."

"Maybe, but only because Matthew hasn't figured out a way to get it. But he will. You can count on it."

"It's really not an issue. Not that it's any of your business, but Matt Hanson is not in my life."

"Then why is he here tonight?"

"Because he hasn't learned the meaning of the word *no*." The devil in Jenny stirred. She couldn't resist a taunt. "Or maybe he heard you were going to be here."

"It's possible." Krystal flipped her golden hair over her shoulder and struck a seductive pose. "He always was drawn to me, like a moth to a flame."

And got burned for his trouble. Jenny almost felt sorry for Matt.

"You know, you should be thanking me," Krystal said in a haughty tone. "I was the one who talked Matthew into doing the sperm thing. If you play your cards right, you could be set for life."

"Don't you think that if I believed this baby was Matt's I'd marry him in a minute?" Jenny asked pointedly, certain Krystal wouldn't catch onto her sarcasm, or that she was playing fast and loose with the truth. "That I'd be happy to trap someone like him, someone smart and handsome, who so obviously wants to be a father?"

Krystal seemed perplexed for a moment, as if it had never occurred to her that anyone would marry for reasons other than money. While she was obviously not the brightest bulb in the box, she was vicious and, Jenny guessed, dangerous.

"It doesn't really matter, does it?" the awful woman said finally. "What you want, I mean. Matthew believes that kid is his. He wants it and he doesn't care who he has to step on to get it."

Krystal sailed away, seemingly convinced she'd scored some kind of coup de grâce over Jenny. It was a good thing she left when she did. If she'd called Alexis *it* one more time Jenny would have pulled her bleached blonde hair out by the roots.

When he looked at Krystal with his eyes and not his hormones, Matt could see he'd mistaken flash for substance, and that sex, no matter how hot, was not love.

He thought of holding Jenny in his arms and rubbing her sore back and decided he wouldn't trade that moment, or either of their brief kisses, for any amount of time with any other woman.

He shook his head in disbelief. He was *not* falling in love with Jenny Ames. She was sweet, although exasperating, but nothing more. She was merely the vessel carrying his child, the means to an end he desired. They would come to terms, seal their deal, then they'd part as friends. They could do it for the sake of the child, right?

But if that was such a good thing, why did the idea bother him so much?

He wished the dinner would start, that they could eat, make nice and then get the heck out of here. His eyes scanned the room for Jenny, but Krystal's approach blocked his view.

"Hello, Krystal," he said dryly. "What brings you out tonight?"

"Just seeing how the other half lives. Not quite your usual style, is it, Matthew."

"Oh, I don't know. Maybe I'm beginning to see the world through new eyes."

"And might Miss Jenny Ames be responsible for that?"

"My relationship with Jenny is none of your business."

"She says there is no relationship. She says you're not in her life. Does that mean you're not in her bed, either?"

"That, also, is none of your business."

"Is that why you're so…tense?" She slipped a hand into the opening of his jacket. "I could take care of that for you, Matthew."

She leaned forward to press her slender body against him. Matt was stunned.

He felt nothing.

A woman purported to be one of the most beautiful in the world was coming on to him like gangbusters and he felt nothing. Jenny Ames had only to look down her pert little nose and tell him to get lost and he was hard as the Italian marble on the floor of his foyer.

Go figure.

"We were always very good together, remember?"

"What are you getting at?"

"We could try again, if you wanted to."

She dropped her head and looked up at him through heavily mascaraed lashes. Matt nearly laughed.

"I underestimated how much you wanted a baby and

I'm very sorry about the misunderstanding. I would be willing to get pregnant if that's what you really want."

"Krystal," he said softly. "This is a big step for you and I can see you've given it a lot of thought." He looked into her eyes and saw in them the gleam of triumph. "I appreciate the offer, but I could never live with myself if I were the one responsible for making you *fat!*"

Krystal rose to her full height, plus heels, and snorted—not an attractive thing. "Holding grudges is not a very endearing attribute, Matthew."

"Perhaps not, but I guess we'll have to live with it. In the meantime, stay away from me and leave Jenny alone."

Krystal spun on her heel, tottered for a second, then regained her balance and headed for the door, leaving her escort in shock only a few feet away.

"I'm sorry you had to see that, Trev," Matt apologized.

"Not at all. It was very entertaining. And educational. I should have known something was up when she called and asked if she could accompany me tonight. I can see now why you kicked her to the curb."

"There was no kicking involved. She and I had a disagreement about family planning, that's all."

He must have seen Matt's eyes scan the room and light on Jenny, because when Matt turned back to his friend, Trevor was smiling.

"Are you the father of Jenny's child?"

"There seems to be some disagreement on that, too. We won't know until the baby's born and the hospital does some blood tests." Assuming Jenny would allow blood tests. "Until then, I'm, uh, taking an interest in her welfare."

"Jenny has a lot of friends among the board members and in the community. I'd be careful, if I were you."

"Is that a warning, old friend?"

Trevor pinned Matt with a look that would have made a lesser man cower. "Sounded like one to me," he said, walking away.

Matt Hanson was a beast, a rotten mean-spirited excuse for a human being, whom she would never forgive for ruining her special evening.

He'd stood in the corner, glaring at her, silently criticizing her every move and making her feel as though nothing she did was right.

"I'm impressed," he said later as he guided her toward the door. "You were magnificent up there, in your pretty dress, playing Lady Bountiful."

"I wasn't playing." She stopped midstride, amazed that the people he'd met and the things he'd heard hadn't gotten through to him. "The foundation does good work, regardless of what you think. The people we honored give ceaselessly to the community and they deserved their special night. What we did here was important. You just don't want to admit it."

"Oh, yeah," he said, his voice dripping with sarcasm and some unnamed anger she couldn't identify. "Sending a single mother to the doctor in a chauffeured limousine is real important work."

"She wasn't—" Jenny exhaled her hurt and frustration in a furious huff. "You don't get it do you? You know, Matt, there's a real world outside your swanky office, away from your gated-community mansion. A world where people help each other without thinking about the return on their investment."

"Hey, honey. I call 'em as I see 'em. And so far, all I've seen is a lot of people patting themselves on the back."

Jenny's eyes nearly popped out of her head as she gasped her outrage. Anger battled with propriety as she debated whether or not to slug him in the nose right there in the middle of the crowded banquet room. Instead, she opened her evening bag and dug around, sorting through its meager contents. She pulled out a pen and pad, scribbled briefly, then ripped out the page and handed it to Matt.

"Meet me at this address at nine in the morning. And don't you dare be late." She repacked her purse and snapped it shut.

"What is this?"

"It's me, Matt. It's what I stand for. And once and for all, if you don't like it, you can—" she pressed her lips together as she searched for the perfect rebuke "—lump it."

Matt stared at her, obviously stunned. Jenny took a breath, squared her shoulders and turned to walk away. "Dr. Barnes is leaving. I need to thank him for coming. Ask Mr. Steadman to take you home. I have friends here. One of them will give me a ride."

Matt grabbed her arm.

"Hold on a minute, wildcat. I'm your escort for the evening, and I'm not leaving without you." He tucked her hand into the curve of his elbow.

She pulled away. "I don't want you for an escort anymore. You're excused…permanently."

For a moment they wrestled for possession of her hand. When he captured her chin with his strong fingers and turned her face to his, she ceased struggling.

"I spoke without thinking, Jenny. I wasn't making fun."

His apology beat inside her head in time with the pounding of her heart. Tears pooled at the corners of her eyes. God, she hated that he could hurt her with his words. A single tear slipped out and began its journey down her cheek. She blocked his hand as he reached for her, blotting her skin with the back of her hand.

"Don't cry. I didn't mean to criticize."

"Then why did you? This is the very reason I don't like to be around you. You're harsh and judgmental. You go from Mr. Congeniality to Mr. T in the space of a nanosecond and I never know what's set you off!"

Matt's face mirrored his shock. Even through the fog of her anger, she could tell he was surprised she had dared to criticize him.

"Maybe you're right. I'm usually a levelheaded kind of guy, but sometimes you just plain tie me in knots. It's not your fault."

"I know it's not my fault. If you've got some kind of personality defect, I don't want to know about it. You never cease to surprise me. You make fun of people and things you don't understand."

"Then help me understand. I want to know more about the charities and why they're so important to you."

"I'll think about it. But don't be too hopeful. I don't like you or your crowd."

He clearly didn't like that comment. His eyes narrowed menacingly.

"What did Krystal say to you?"

"Nothing."

"I doubt that. Krystal never could keep her opinions to herself."

"Nothing important, then."

"If she did say something to upset you, you'd tell me, wouldn't you?"

"I've told you everything you need to know."

"Have you?" His voice was so knowing, his question

so penetrating, it shook her to the core. She had secrets, what woman didn't? But mostly hers were sins of omission, not commission. Of lack, not excess.

She turned away. "I think it's time for you to go."

"I'm not leaving you here by yourself."

"Look around you, Hanson. I won't be by myself."

"I mean without me, Jenny. I'm not leaving here without you." The look in his eyes warned her not to argue, as if she thought that would do any good. "Introduce me to Dr. Barnes, okay?"

Jenny acquiesced, unwilling to make a scene, but it was not over. He had to learn, once and for all, that she was not a woman to be trifled with, that she was smarter than Krystal McDonnough and every bit as determined as Matt to get what she wanted.

It was a silent ride back to Jenny's house. Matt talked, she answered in monosyllables, still angry and unwilling to admit that his jibes about her work being a joke hurt her deeply.

And then there was Krystal. Her threats and accusations left Jenny unsettled, not really frightened, but no longer confident that Matt would be so easily bored and therefore dispatched.

The way Krystal draped herself over Matt, and the way he let her, spoke volumes, and Jenny could not ignore the noise.

Always the gentleman, Matt saw Jenny to her door. She clutched her small purse in her hands and kept them hidden beneath the luxurious fabric of the wrap Matt had given her. How, she wondered, could someone be so caring one moment and such a blockhead the next?

She looked up at him towering annoyingly over her. It had been a tiring evening, she was this close to collapsing in her bed and he was…oh, dear Lord…he was looking at her like she was Cherries Jubilee.

There was an unmistakable glow of appreciation in his eyes when she shifted the soft, bulky collar around her neck. Jenny shivered. She didn't want him to look at her like that. Her heart twisted painfully. She'd seen him look at Krystal that same way.

"You look very beautiful tonight…very sexy. I couldn't keep my eyes off you all night."

Suddenly she realized his words were just that— mouth music to guarantee he'd get what he wanted.

An inelegant sputter burst from her lips. "You must need glasses if you think a woman who waddles like a duck is sexy."

"You don't accept compliments very easily, do you? Most of the women I've known act as if praise is their right by law."

"Was Krystal like that?"

He stroked her hair with the tips of his fingers, leaning forward to kiss her cheek. "I don't particularly want to talk about her right how."

"She must have loved you very much to be so upset over losing you," Jenny persisted.

"Krystal McDonnough never loved anyone but herself. Never loved any*thing* but money."

"You're so cynical. You think of everything in terms of what can be bought and sold."

He slipped his fingers through the strands of her hair to cup the back of her head. "Not tonight."

With a little sigh she relaxed into him, knowing it wasn't the best idea she'd had all day but helpless to refuse the comfort his nearness promised. Like the time in her office, the needs of her soul took over, and the warnings in her head receded.

She hadn't reckoned on this, the loneliness and the need, when she'd developed her carefully constructed life plan. No man for her bed, no father for her child. No touches to make her shiver and burn, ache and sigh, all at once.

"Can I kiss you good-night?"

The question startled her and, to her relief, gave her a chance to emerge from the stupor Matt's touch engendered. "I don't think that would be a good idea."

"Why not? We're friends, aren't we? I want to kiss you."

"Do you always do what you want?"

Matt's smile said it all. She had no trouble translating. *Yeah. Always do what I like, always get what I want.*

She took a step back and he took one forward, closing the momentary gap between them. When she opened her mouth to protest, he swooped in for his kiss.

The touch of his mouth on hers was so soft and fleeting she thought her heart would flutter its way out of her chest. He lifted his head and pinned her with that same look of possession she remembered from the day they met.

"When you were eating dessert you got a little dot of whipped cream on your lip right here…" He briefly touched the peak of her upper lip with the tip of his tongue. "I almost jumped across the table I wanted so badly to be the one to lick it off."

He eased her a little closer into his arms then leaned forward to whisper into her ear. She backed up and shivered as cool air surged between them. He grinned, as though he thought he had her where he wanted her. Little did he know that what she wanted was to run. As far and as fast as her pregnant body could waddle.

"Can I come in?"

She shook her head. "I don't think that would be a good idea." Maybe if she said it enough times, she'd begin to believe it.

"Why not?" he growled, obviously on edge again.

Krystal's words echoed in her head. Matthew hadn't pressed his case this way before, or tried to seduce her to get what he wanted. While Jenny wouldn't admit to an actual feeling of fear, a little space and serious thought might not be amiss.

"I'm not sure I want to get involved with you."

For the first time, he laid his hands on her belly. Always the obliging little lady, Alexis shifted, and Jenny knew Matt felt the movement. He smiled and adjusted the placement of his fingers, pressing them gently into her flesh with a touch that was at the same time bold and tender.

"Don't you think that's a little like locking the barn door after the horses get out? We're already involved, as involved as a man and a woman can get."

The way he said it—a man and a woman—was so deeply sexual and so sweetly intimate it almost made Jenny give in and open the door—to her heart as well as her house. Almost.

The old protest that she didn't accept that the baby was his died on her lips. Instead she shook her head.

Matt waited quietly while her inner argument raged. "You know I'm right, Jenny. Tell me something. How many times were you inseminated before you got pregnant?"

Shocked by the question, Jenny lifted her face to him. She knew he could see her blush, even in the faint glow of the porch light.

"You know it was only the one time."

Matt smiled that self-satisfied smile she hated, the one that said he thought he was about to score big over an opponent.

"See? We're so potent together even Mother Nature knows it. My little buckaroos drew a bead on your egg and *bam,* instant baby. Hey, I'm surprised you're not carrying twins."

Jenny couldn't argue with that. She'd gone to the clinic fourteen days into her cycle, had been insemi-nated once and knew a mere two weeks later, when she missed her regular as clockwork period, that her dream of having a child of her own was about to come true.

But could sperm be as aggressive and determined as their donor?

She definitely didn't want to think about that. Her mind was too full of the image of Krystal and Matt at the party, the beautiful model pressing her slender, un-pregnant body against Matt's, and poor Mr. Quinn standing there with his mouth hanging open.

It was proof positive that Matt was still attracted to his ex, regardless of his protestations to the contrary.

Jenny knew she couldn't compete and didn't want to. She knew a lost cause when she saw one. And she knew the only reason Matt was with her at that moment was because of the baby. If Krystal had wanted his child, Jenny never would have met Matt, wouldn't be pregnant with his child now. There would have been no Hanson sperm and no mistake.

He was with her because of the baby.

The kisses were not real. The concern was not real. It was all only about the baby.

Her heart dipped a little, stirring memories of other disappointments, other slights. Then the anger rose.

She would not let it hurt. She would not.

"It's cold," she said testily, using her hand to push him away, "and I'm tired. My shoes are pinching me and I'm in no mood to debate the miracle of procreation."

"If you'd let me in I could rub those feet for you."

"Mr. Steadman is waiting."

"He won't mind. He thinks you're the ultimate in genteel womanhood. His words."

"Let's keep it that way," she said sharply, jabbing the key into its lock.

"Tomorrow morning?" he asked.

She glanced back over her shoulder and saw him standing with his hands in the pockets of his custom-made tuxedo slacks. The white silk scarf he'd tossed carelessly around his neck glimmered in the light from her living room window.

There was a Gatsbyesque quality about him that sent a bolt of longing streaking through her body, from the tips of her breasts to the skin on her belly he'd touched so tenderly, to the woman-place deep inside her that ached to know him.

He was heartbreakingly handsome, supremely confident and scarier than any monster she'd ever imagined under her bed. And here she was giving him a toehold into one of the most precious and private parts of her life.

"No," she said. "I've changed my mind. You're off the hook."

"Really? Now I'm curious. What could Jenny be hiding on Crandall Street that she doesn't want Matt to know about?"

He backed away, turning just as he reached the edge of the porch, then loped down the steps toward the car.

"See you in the morning, Genevieve."

Chapter Seven

When Jenny handed him the slip of paper bearing only an address and declared *this* was who she was, Matt had been completely thrown off balance.

Yet, as he stood in front of the shabby brownstone in a once fashionable Cincinnati neighborhood, staring at the sign that read Hope's House, understanding dawned.

He remembered the controversy that swirled about the community when the center for teen mothers and their drug-addicted babies was proposed. He'd thrust it from his consciousness, choosing instead to concentrate on business and what he now knew was his doomed relationship with Krystal.

Jenny obviously hadn't swept it from her life, though. Matt would have bet his last dollar she was up to her pretty knees in support of the charity.

Of course she was. The house was full of babies. Where else would she be so completely in her element?

The director greeted him by name as he stepped through the door and wasted no time thanking him for providing transportation to the doctor for herself and the baby who'd been ill.

Matt made a mental note to apologize to Jenny for the stupid "unwed mother" remark he'd made the night before. Even after considerable reflection he still couldn't figure out what had made him act like such a jerk. Maybe it was the shock of seeing Jenny in such close proximity to Krystal, or perhaps it was the realization that Jenny was a part of a larger world; that she had friends and obligations outside his realm of influence.

No matter how vigorously he'd denied that he wanted her for himself, he had to recognize that she had other interests and responsibilities. He would have to take his place at the end of a very long line.

And somehow, he didn't like that very much.

Maggie Turner interrupted his thoughts. "I didn't know you were interested in our work."

"To be perfectly honest, Ms. Turner, until General Ames over there ordered me here, I really wasn't aware of your existence. Of course I remember the publicity during the zoning process, but beyond that I have to admit I'm pretty clueless about Hope's House."

"Call me Maggie. What we have here is your everyday halfway house for young moms and infants recovering from drug addiction. As soon as the babies are well enough to leave the hospital and the moms are over the worst part of their recovery, they meet up here at the center. Then the real work starts."

They walked to the back of the living/dining area to a low bookshelf that held an encyclopedia, a couple of well-thumbed Dr. Spock's and a set of GED test books.

"Before a client is approved for the center she has to sign an agreement that she will go to class at least four hours a day to prepare for, then take, the GED. She also attends classes on life skills like cooking, budgeting and household management. She does homework, housework, the whole nine yards."

"Sounds like boot camp."

Maggie laughed heartily. From the corner of his eye Matt saw Jenny look up and smile. He fought the urge to bound across the room like an overexcited large-breed puppy, to beg for more of her smiles.

"I've heard that before," Maggie said, laughing again. "But seriously, these are young women who haven't had a lot of success in their lives. None are married, nor do they have any expectation of finding a stable, loving relationship. We try to give them the time, the education and the confidence to believe anything is possible for them."

"How long does all that take?"

"There's no timetable. Every day is a struggle when you're this young and have so many strikes against you."

"Where do you get the funding to operate?"

"We do it all on grants. Some from the city, the county and the state. Some from foundations, like the Prescott. We also have some individual donors. I hope you'll become one."

They made the rounds of the ground floor, once passing by Jenny in the nursery area. She was holding a wriggling, blue-swathed baby, just as he imagined she would hold his baby. He watched as she paced and patted and hummed to the tiny, squalling bundle and marveled at the patience and love she exhibited.

He wondered what it would be like to be the recipient of that love, and felt, for a moment, the sweet ache of longing.

Longing for a wife and baby of his own.

A wife like Jenny and a baby named Alexis.

At the bottom of a flight of stairs that ran up one side of the enormous entry hall, Maggie paused. "The girls' rooms are upstairs, no men allowed. We have a laying-in system where the children sleep in the rooms with their mothers each night."

"Where are they this morning?"

Maggie arched an eyebrow. "They're at church, Mr. Hanson. Nondenominational, of course."

Matt suppressed a grin. "Of course."

"How do you know Jenny?"

"She didn't tell you?"

"No."

"I'm the baby's father."

"Jenny's baby?"

"None other."

"Oh. I didn't mean to pry. Jenny never said anything…I didn't know she'd met anybody."

"We only met about a month ago."

"Then how—" She clamped her hand over her mouth. "I'm sorry," she mumbled around her fingers, then dropped her hand to rest on her chest. "I have more questions than sense."

"That's okay, but I'm going to let Jenny answer them. I think I've already said too much."

"Don't worry. Your secrets, whatever they may be, are safe with me. I think of Jenny as a daughter…or perhaps a much, much younger sister." She laughed, and her gray curls bounced. "I'd never betray a confidence. Now, where were we?"

"How long has Jenny been volunteering?"

"Since the center opened. We stole her away from the neonatal unit at University Hospital."

"She volunteered there?"

"She volunteers everywhere. I've never seen a more tireless worker. If only all our helpers were like her. I take it you haven't seen her in action?"

"No." He'd dropped her off at work and picked her up after work but he realized he'd never shown any interest *in* her work.

"She's like a whirlwind." Maggie smiled. "Or maybe more like an octopus, trying to spread out her tentacles to help wherever she can."

"How can I help?" It was almost a relief to find a place where his money could do some real good. "What are your most pressing needs?"

"That's easy. Food, diapers and volunteers."

"The food and diapers I can do. Is it all right if my assistant calls you in the morning? You can tell her what you need and we'll see that you get it."

"What about the volunteers?"

"That may take a little more work."

"What about you?"

Matt grinned. "When does Jenny come in?"

"Every Sunday morning at nine o'clock."

"Doesn't she go to church?"

"Ensuring happy childhoods is Jenny's religion."

Matt grinned, feeling a lightness of spirit he hadn't known in months. "Then I guess I'll see you next Sunday."

"What were you and Maggie talking about?" Jenny asked when Matt caught up with her in the center's kitchen.

"This house. The babies. You."

"In that order?" She laughed, and he thought he'd never heard such a beautiful sound. "I'm glad to see you're finally getting some balance in your life."

For a moment he was paralyzed by the sight of her smile—usually so elusive—and the minuscule dimples that appeared in her cheeks. It was like being struck by lightning, only, unlike the typical lightning victim, he wanted to feel the impact again and again.

"Well," he drawled, "you've thrown me for a loop, that's for sure."

"I didn't mean to." She leaned over the counter to place several formula bottles near the sink. Her baby-rocking exertions had put a glow in her cheeks that nearly matched the pink top she wore with faded jeans. She looked impossibly young and innocent. "To be perfectly honest, I never gave any thought to how the sperm donor felt about what happened after he…well, you know."

Matt froze. Was she saying that she thought he was the baby's father? Admitting that what he'd said all along was true?

She continued nervously, as though she could read his thoughts. "Most of the Morningstar's donors are students from the medical school at the University of Cincinnati. That's what I'd hoped for—somebody scholarly and altruistic, aware of the needs of the larger world."

"And you think I'm not those things?"

"I didn't say that. I really don't know you well enough to judge. You've been very generous to me and I appreciate it, but there are so many other people out there with needs greater than mine."

"Are you saying that if I was as generous to the other people out there, you'd like me better?"

"No, you'd like you better."

"I'm not some kind of miser who spends his evenings counting his gold, you know. I have philanthropic interests. A couple of years ago I was approached to sit on the United Way board."

"That's nice, but what are you doing now?"

Matt crossed his arms over his chest and scowled. Did he really need this impertinent little pumpkin pointing these things out to him?

"I'm not criticizing you. I'm only trying to show you that we're very different people—"

"Well, I hope so."

"You know what I mean. We have completely opposite goals and are following divergent paths in life."

"Baloney. You just admitted you don't know me very well." He reached over and touched her arm. "Spend some time with me and let me show you who I am. Have dinner with me at my place tonight."

"No." She pulled away.

"Why not?"

"Dinner is too personal." Jenny picked up a towel and began to dry her hands. She dropped her gaze, and her voice softened. "Besides, the last dinner we had together didn't turn out very well, and I don't want to repeat it."

"If you won't come to my house, come to my office. Tomorrow. I've learned about your job, now you can learn about mine. Meet my staff and maybe they can convince you what a good guy I am."

"Do they think you're a good guy?"

"I like to think so."

"When was the last time you did something nice for them just because?"

Matt raised an eyebrow. "Because?"

"Because they work hard and make you rich. Because people like surprises. Because you can."

"I don't know. I'll have to think about it."

Jenny's eyes sparkled. She was clearly enjoying her teasing. "If you have to think about it, it's been too long."

Matt expelled a frustrated, irritated snort. "When was the last time you did something nice for Nancy?"

She didn't even have to think about it. Somehow that irritated him.

"Nancy is the ultimate poetry lover. She can quote almost any American poet you can name. Last week at the library I went into the Friends' shop and found an old volume of Carl Sandburg's works. It was in good shape, with gold edging on the paper. It cost me two dollars and she was thrilled with it."

"You bought her a used book?" He thought of the library full of signed first editions he'd inherited from his father. And Jenny was getting all excited over a book-sale find.

"It's the thought that counts, not the score."

"Is that what you think? That I'm keeping score?"

"No, not really." She placed a large pot in the sink and turned on the water. "I guess it's true what they say. Money's not an issue unless you don't have any."

"And I do and you don't and never the twain shall meet, right?"

She shut off the water and started to lift the heavy pot. Matt reached around her to take it. She pointed to the stove, and he placed it on the burner.

"You still don't understand."

A sound came from the front of the house, and Matt recognized it as baby laughter.

"Come with me," Jenny said, reaching for his hand. "I think it's time you met the proprietor of Hope's House."

Maggie stood in the living room, waiting for them. Jenny tightened her grip on Matt's hand as she dropped to her knees in front of her friend.

"Good morning, little love," she crooned. At first Matt was confused by the tone of Jenny's voice and by the fact that she seemed to be talking to Maggie's knees. Then, as he watched, a small child emerged, bit by bit, from behind the older woman's denim-clad legs.

"How's my girlfriend today?" Jenny asked.

The little girl, dressed in the same pink Jenny wore and wearing the smallest pair of sneakers he'd ever seen, completely ignored Jenny, and instead, locked her gaze on Matt.

Matt smiled at the child, encouraging her to come out from her hiding place. She tilted her head back to look at him and briefly lost her balance, recovering only after holding out her tiny hands to steady herself. Matt couldn't help smiling at the concentration it took for her to keep her dainty feet firmly on the ground.

She walked slowly toward Matt, never taking her eyes from his. Matt was stunned at the perfection of the miniature person, at the reality that stood before him.

Before, he'd only thought of Alexis as the baby in her mother's belly. Now it hit him full force that he'd neglected to consider the child as a walking, talking, breathing entity who would take first steps, speak first words, go to school, learn to drive.

Date.

He made a mental note to check on the legality of using a shotgun to run off unwelcome suitors.

The child stopped in front of him and again tilted her head to get a better look. She studied him as carefully as any business contact he'd ever had. When he looked into her dark eyes he saw an intelligence he never considered possible in a child.

She lifted her arms. "Up," she commanded.

Matt lifted her into his arms and she settled into the crook of his elbow with a bounce. Brown curls tumbled into her eyes and she brushed them away with her fingers, as he'd seen Jenny do. Just as Alexis would do when she reached this age.

"Matt, I'd like you to meet Miss Hope Turner. Hope, this is my friend, Matt.

"Maaa," Hope said, nodding, apparently convinced she'd gotten it right. Then she pointed at Jenny. "Ninny," she said.

"Turner?" Matt asked, peering around the child's small head.

"Hope is Maggie's daughter."

Matt's eyes moved from the brown-skinned child to Maggie's porcelain complexion and back again.

"I adopted Hope about two years ago," Maggie explained. "She was abandoned at the hospital. Her mother thought she'd be handicapped because of the drug use."

"Is she? Handicapped, I mean?" he asked softly, terrified of what the answer might be.

"No, she's normal. She's one of the lucky ones."

"Maggie finalized the adoption and changed the name of the center all in the same week," Jenny added.

"And never looked back."

Hope clearly didn't like being ignored while the conversation spun on around her. She patted Matt's cheek, then pointed at her foot.

"Shoes," she announced.

"Yes," Matt agreed. "They're very pretty."

Hope nodded. "Pitty," she echoed, and then and there, Matt fell in love.

He was sure he looked like a dope, holding the little girl and having a conversation about her footwear, yet he couldn't have cared less.

"Uh-oh," he heard Maggie say. "She's made another conquest."

"Yep," Jenny replied with a laugh. "The bigger they are, the harder they fall."

Yeah, he'd fallen, all right. Fallen headfirst in love with fatherhood. And he didn't care if he ever got up.

Jenny watched as Maggie took Hope from Matt's arms and turned toward the kitchen, announcing lunchtime. Jenny clutched Matt's hand and he helped her rise. She turned away from him, using her fingertips to brush tears from her cheeks.

The day Jenny began volunteering at the center she promised herself she would never cry in front of the children; that they would never hear the catch in her voice that heralded tears, that they would only feel love and never pity.

Rarely was it an easy promise to keep, especially on days like this when Alexis was so active and her emotions were so raw it seemed they lay right on the surface. Jenny could almost feel the baby's heart beating in tandem with her own.

It was ironic that today, of all days, when she truly envisioned what Matt would be like as a father, that her tears had gotten the best of her. She should have been happy, but her heart was breaking.

Now that she knew the truth, had seen Matt with a child in his arms and imagined that child was Alexis, how could she keep his daughter away from him?

"Our baby will be strong and healthy, too," he said quietly from behind her.

Jenny turned and rested her head on Matt's chest. She could hear his heartbeat as clearly as that of the child in her womb. "And beautiful."

He dropped a kiss on the top of her head. "Hmmm?"

"Alexis will be beautiful."

Behind them the front door burst open. The sound of feminine laughter drifted in from the living room.

"The girls are back." She stepped away from Matt and smiled, holding out her hand for the handkerchief he always carried. Of course, this time he had to struggle a little to wrench it from the back pocket of his tight jeans. She glanced away, praying he hadn't seen her watching him.

But he had noticed, she realized. And he smiled, a wry, sexy smile that held a hint of melancholy. It made her temperature rise and her insides do a little flip-flop that had little to do with Lexie's future career as a gymnast.

They stood, frozen into place amid the mismatched cribs and stacks of faded baby clothes, oblivious to the various squeals, cries and coos of the babies around them. She raised her gaze to meet his. The chocolate eyes that had mesmerized her from the moment they'd met held a promise that had less to do with caring for babies and more to do with making them from scratch.

Jenny swallowed roughly, struggling to break the spell he cast merely by looking at her. "Can you stay for lunch?"

He shook his head. "I have a lot of work to do, so I'd better go. Steadman will take you home."

Jenny studied the much-too-serious look on Matt's face and frowned. "Are you all right? I didn't mean for any of this to upset you."

"I'm fine." He reached for her, cupping her cheek in his palm. His thumb grazed the corner of her mouth as he leaned forward to place a soft kiss on her lips. "I'm proud of you. You work hard to make a difference, no matter what it takes. You really are an extraordinary woman."

"I'm nothing special."

He smiled, and the warmth of it went straight to her heart. "You are to me."

Back on the street Matt turned to look at the center. The old place needed work. He wondered if there was a construction company out there that would donate the labor if he paid for the supplies. And if there wasn't— what the hell, it was only money.

He figured his checkbook was going to get a work-out in the coming months and realized, with no small amount of shock, that he didn't mind a bit.

Suddenly he knew what he had to do. It wouldn't be easy, and it wouldn't be cheap, but it would be worth it.

If he was going to make the world a better place for his daughter, and the woman he'd come to love, he'd better get on the stick.

It was with a new sense of purpose that he headed for his office.

He'd walked a few blocks toward the city's center by the time the sounds of the neighborhood pierced his consciousness. Young girls bundled up in denim jack-ets filled the sidewalks, double-dutching with their jump ropes. Boys of all sizes and descriptions displayed their mastery of basketball and skateboarding, their breaths puffing out condensation like cartoon dialogue balloons. Small shops dotted the street; a bookstore here, a family-style restaurant there.

A small church, likely the nondenominational one the center's residents attended earlier, advertised a bake sale. The smell of fresh-baked bread drew him through the cracked and peeling basement door. He was greeted like a neighbor and treated to tastes of nearly every item on sale, leaving only after he'd bought every chocolate chip cookie in the place.

Resuming his walk toward the office, Matt picked up his pace as the crisp fall breeze turned into a frigid wind. Glad he'd left Steadman to take Jenny home, he nevertheless rethought his decision to go by foot and began looking for a cab. It being a lazy Sunday morning, none presented itself. He headed for a group of people waiting at a bus stop.

When he had to flip his collar up to keep his ears from freezing, he thought of Jenny, waiting for the bus in a coat that didn't button up all the way. At least he'd been able to do that much for her; getting her off the sidewalk and into a warm car might not count for much in her estimation, but it gave him satisfaction.

Then it hit him. He stopped in his tracks and felt a smile working its way across his nearly frozen face.

When he'd referred to the baby as "theirs," she hadn't argued.

Now *that* was progress.

Chapter Eight

Jenny pressed the elevator call button, then looked up at the panel that numbered the floors, one through twenty-four. Matt's office was on the seventeenth floor.

Wasn't seventeen her unlucky number? The elevator doors swished open, and she hesitated, although not long enough for the doors to close. She stepped on, alone, leaving the strangely silent lobby behind.

She hadn't realized she'd agreed to this little visit until Matt reminded her of it when he'd called for her that morning. She tried to demur but he, as usual, wasn't having any of it. Quid pro quo, he'd called it. So here she was, surprised he hadn't met her at the curb to drag her inside.

What did he want? The question nagged. Jenny rested a hand on her belly and thought of life without Alexis. No man could be that callous, could he?

She struggled to reconcile what she knew firsthand and

what she'd heard. He made no secret of his interest in her well-being. He'd shown a generous side that surprised her. Had her suspicions blinded her to his good points?

In an effort to buy more time she punched the button marked seven, then, like a mischievous child, let her fingers walk, one over the other, all the way up the board. It would slow things down long enough for her to think. Long enough to plan an escape better than the one where she walked down eight, nine, ten flights of stairs.

The problem—her dilemma—was that she was falling in love with Matt Hanson. It had started the moment he'd lifted tiny Hope Turner into his arms and she'd imagined it was Alexis instead. It was a strange, wonderful, scary thing, especially in light of her suspicions about his intentions toward her baby.

Most especially when the chances of him ever loving her in return were so astronomically outrageous not even a NASA engineer could calculate them.

Every night before she wished Lexie sweet dreams and closed her eyes she swore to herself that tomorrow, always tomorrow, she would tell Matt she couldn't see him again, that things were too unsettled and life too uncertain to go buying trouble.

And every morning when she opened the door to him she begged the fates for one more day.

And so, here she was on an elevator, climbing inexorably, one floor at a time, straight into heartbreak's lair.

Ego. It was ego, pure and simple, that had brought her here. He wanted her to meet his staff and she couldn't resist poking her nose into his business, just to make sure his employees were happy and would continue to watch over him after she was gone.

"You've lost your mind," she chided, affection and

GET FREE BOOKS and a FREE GIFT WHEN YOU PLAY THE...

Just scratch off the silver box with a coin. Then check below to see the gifts you get!

SLOT MACHINE GAME!

YES! I have scratched off the silver box. Please send me the 2 free Silhouette Romance® books and gift for which I qualify. I understand I am under no obligation to purchase any books, as explained on the back of this card.

310 SDL D7WR   210 SDL D7W5

FIRST NAME   LAST NAME

ADDRESS

APT.#   CITY

STATE/ PROV.   ZIP/POSTAL CODE

7	7	7	**Worth TWO FREE BOOKS plus a BONUS Mystery Gift!**
♪	♪	♪	**Worth TWO FREE BOOKS!**
♣	♣	♣	**Worth ONE FREE BOOK!**
🔔	🔔	♪	**TRY AGAIN!**

www.eHarlequin.com

(S-R-06/05)

Offer limited to one per household and not valid to current Silhouette Romance® subscribers. All orders subject to approval.

© 2000 HARLEQUIN ENTERPRISES LTD. ® and TM are trademarks owned and used by the trademark owner and/or its licensee.

DETACH AND MAIL CARD TODAY!

The Silhouette Reader Service™ — Here's how it works:

Accepting your 2 free books and gift places you under no obligation to buy anything. You may keep the books and gift and return the shipping statement marked "cancel." If you do not cancel, about a month later we'll send you 4 additional books and bill you just $3.57 each in the U.S., or $4.05 each in Canada, plus 25¢ shipping & handling per book and applicable taxes if any.* That's the complete price and — compared to cover prices of $4.25 each in the U.S. and $4.99 each in Canada — it's quite a bargain! You may cancel at any time, but if you choose to continue, every month we'll send you 4 more books, which you may either purchase at the discount price or return to us and cancel your subscription.

*Terms and prices subject to change without notice. Sales tax applicable in N.Y. Canadian residents will be charged applicable provincial taxes and GST. Credit or debit balances in a customer's account(s) may be offset by any other outstanding balance owed by or to the customer.

If offer card is missing write to: Silhouette Reader Service, 3010 Walden Ave., P.O. Box 1867, Buffalo NY 14240-1867

BUSINESS REPLY MAIL
FIRST-CLASS MAIL   PERMIT NO. 717-003   BUFFALO, NY

POSTAGE WILL BE PAID BY ADDRESSEE

SILHOUETTE READER SERVICE
3010 WALDEN AVE
PO BOX 1867
BUFFALO NY 14240-9952

NO POSTAGE
NECESSARY
IF MAILED
IN THE
UNITED STATES

suspicion battling hope and fear. The last thing in the world Matthew Robert Hanson, millionaire babe magnet, needed was Jenny Ames worrying about him.

But that didn't make her stop. Nothing would ever make her stop.

She closed her eyes and leaned against the wall, willing the knowledge not to hurt.

Swish, open.

"Jenny? Are you all right?" The voice, when it came out of the dark, was smooth as silk.

Before she opened her eyes she admitted what had suddenly become her truth.

Not "falling." Fallen.

She had fallen in love with Matt Hanson. With his kindness and his generosity. And his stubborn streak, so like her own. She had to believe, had to trust, that he wouldn't hurt her. It wouldn't be easy, but it was important, for Alexis and for herself, for today and for the future, that she try.

He'd stepped on the elevator and patiently waited for her to open her eyes and answer his question. She did so willingly, the warmth of him wrapping itself around her heart.

"Jenny?"

"Matt."

He moved forward and took her in his arms, smoothly, almost as though he'd been waiting on the other side of the door for her to appear and make his life complete. There was no hesitation in his touch, as if he'd decided, much as she had, that the time for waiting and wondering and worrying and questioning had ended.

"How are my girls this afternoon?" Matt rubbed his palms over her belly, his long-fingered hands gentle, his touch possessive. The cashmere cape she'd draped over her arm fell soundlessly to the floor.

The elevator began to move upward, taking them toward the top floor. She hadn't seen Matt press the button, but considered the possibility that he'd used the same magic on the elevator he used on her.

"We're fine."

"No more gymnastics?" he asked, in a voice as soft and comforting as a down pillow, one she wanted to snuggle into for more than just a moment. Forever, maybe?

Jenny shook her head. "Just a little ballet. A few pirouettes, but no leaps or *tours jetès*."

One of Lexie's tiny limbs shifted and Matt caught the movement with his hands.

"I love it when she moves like that. I think she knows me."

"She's getting used to you." Like her mother.

And it was then, somewhere between the seventeenth and twenty-fourth floors of the Hanson Building, Cincinnati, Ohio, U.S.A., that Jenny accepted Matt as Alexis's father.

Just like that. No bells or whistles, no trumpets blaring. Simply acceptance by her mind of what her heart had surely known all along. What her soul had known from the first time he touched her.

Matt laughed softly as the baby moved again. Jenny felt a joy emanating from him, a strange shimmer of emotion that was aphrodisiaclike in its intensity.

Their eyes met, and he smiled, almost as if he could feel the desire, the need that rose inside her. In one smooth movement he brushed his mouth over hers, teasing her lips, starting a fire inside her she knew would be impossible to extinguish. When he moved away, she moved with him, nearly losing her balance, forcing his hands from her belly to rest alongside her breasts.

Her breath quickened. She wanted, needed him to kiss her again. As if he knew both her mind and her heart, he complied with her unspoken request.

Slipping her arms around his neck, she anchored herself for an onslaught of sensations.

Matt didn't disappoint. He devoured her mouth hungrily, tutoring, teasing, pleasing. He seemed to take delight in circling the rim of her mouth with his tongue. He groaned softly as she followed his lead. He nibbled on her upper lip, she sucked playfully on his lower. Her eyes drifted closed again. She was drowning in pleasure.

His hand moved from her side to cup her breast. Desire centered there. She felt the nipple harden in his palm, felt the flesh grow fuller with each caress of his gentle fingers. She gasped, then moaned softly, unable to hide even her smallest reaction from him.

As the elevator moved upward she felt as if she were flying, soaring as never before, as she never dreamed she would. Gasping, he pulled his mouth from hers and buried his face in the curve of her neck, resting his open mouth against the flesh he encountered there. She felt the pounding of his heart against her own.

Swish, open.

Jenny blinked, the harsh light from outside the elevator momentarily blinding her. "Where are we?"

Matt straightened, leaving a moist trail of kisses on her neck. He drew Jenny's hands down from his neck, and kissed them softly.

"It's the observation deck." He shook his head as if to clear it. "Do you want to look at the view?"

Jenny drew in a shaky breath, then another, head spinning, heart racing, hormones pumping. "No, I think I've experienced enough of the city's amazing natural wonders for one day."

Matt's eyes widened. A dazzling smile transformed his face. "You think I'm amazing?"

"Well, I…"

"I mean, I've been told I'm a good kisser, but no one ever called me amazing."

He reached behind and waved a hand at the elevator panel. *Swish, close.* She didn't actually see his finger meet the button. Maybe he was working his magic again.

"Only good?"

"Hey, I don't mean to brag—"

"You don't?" Jenny couldn't contain her laughter. "Hey, don't get all modest on me. I wouldn't know what to do with an ordinary Matt."

"Very funny, Miss Ames." He dropped one last soft kiss on her lips and took her hand. Both turned to lean against the wall of the elevator. The door opened with a final swish.

Before them stood at least fifty people, of all shapes, sizes and genders. That made one hundred eyes, all trained on Jenny. Maybe that explained the empty lobby.

Matt squeezed her hand. "What do you say we get to work?"

"This was the worst idea I ever had," Matt grumbled. Greg, who stood next to him, smiled benevolently. It made Matt feel like an idiot. "Look at her. Jeez. She's like the Pied Piper. Since she walked in the door, everybody's been following her around like a bunch of love-sick puppies." Yeah, and he was leader of the pack.

Jenny smiled at something one of the secretaries said and he felt himself go hard. Just from her smile. How the mighty have fallen, he thought. "What's Shepherd up to? Does he have to stand so close?"

Greg snickered. "You know they've been dying to meet her ever since they heard about the baby. They're curious, that's all."

"Can't they be curious from a distance?" He squashed the urge to yell at them to back off. Especially the men. Maybe it was because of the way she'd clung to him; maybe it was her pink and swollen lips, her tumbled, well-kissed look that was driving him crazy.

The navy-blue sweater she wore with sexy leggings made his heart race and his blood heat up to volcanic temperatures and beyond. The loose cowl neckline of the sweater tumbled from side to side as she moved, showing more of the ivory expanse of her neck and shoulders than he would like the world to see.

Not that he wouldn't have been perfectly happy to slip her out of that sweater and lay her down on some soft horizontal surface and examine those pretty shoulders and luscious neck himself, especially the little red spot he'd left below her ear.

She kissed like a beginner, but what she lacked in skill she made up for with enthusiasm, making his blood boil with desire. It seemed like hours since they'd stepped off the elevator yet his body was still humming like a well-plucked guitar string.

Simple observation told him she wasn't having any more luck at getting back to normal than he. The sexual electricity they'd created still sparked between them, drawing them toward each other. Like a balloon rubbed against wool, the shimmering attraction just wouldn't stop.

More than once he'd caught her looking at him. She would sip her drink, or tuck her hair behind that sexy little shell of an ear and glance his way.

Then she would blush.

Every time.

Had his staff not surrounded her, he would have dragged her back onto the elevator, closed the door and let good old Mother Nature, or at least his hormones, run wild.

"It's because she's taking an interest in their work," Greg explained, pulling him from his thoughts. "She even asked me about my job, and whether or not I liked working for you."

"I take an interest in their work."

"But do you take an interest in them personally?"

"You sound just like her. I brought them cookies! Hauled them up here from Crandall Street, I might add."

Laughter transformed the lawyer's usually somber face. "That's a good start, but I think your employees would like more. See that woman she's talking to now? Do you know her name?"

"Margaret."

"Margaret what?"

Matt thought for a moment, then conceded defeat. "I don't know."

"Then you probably don't know she has two sons in the army. One is serving in Afghanistan, one in Iraq. Her husband is retired military. He received the Purple Heart for service in the Gulf War. That guy you've been staring daggers at, Shepherd, single-handedly put his younger brother through college and law school."

"Why are you telling me this?"

"So you'll see them as human beings and not autom-atons," Greg said in a tone that made Matt feel like the world's most clueless juror.

He frowned. The old taunt "truth hurts" struck home. "Am I that driven?"

"Man, you give obsessed a bad name."

Matt knew Greg was being honest. Maybe he did put too much emphasis on work, but that didn't mean he didn't care about the people who worked for him. The feeling of obligation to be the same kind of man his father had been was a beacon all during his growing up years. His dad had been both a hard worker and a caring, giving parent. Matt intended to accomplish all that and more.

And between him and his goal stood Jenny Ames.

Or had Jenny become the goal?

Things were changing between them. He'd felt it yes-terday when he'd held her as she'd cried. He'd felt it to-day when she returned his kisses with a passion he felt sure she hadn't shared with anyone else. She was inno-cent, despite the pregnant belly that would lead the world to believe otherwise, but she was no pushover, either. Each and every reaction he saw in her was an honest one.

Even before he'd kissed her he'd felt a softening of her stance, a capitulation, almost, as though she'd de-cided not to fight him anymore.

He felt confident, cocky even, that the prize was within his reach.

Matt rubbed his hands together with relish.

He turned to his friend with a wolfish grin on his face. "Obsessed, huh? See that little woman over there? She's going to change all that."

"How?" Greg asked, suspicion lacing his voice.

"She's going to make me a daddy. She and I and that little baby inside her are going to be a family."

Matt walked Jenny into his office after he'd called a halt to her interviews. He closed the door behind them.

Jenny dropped into a butter-soft leather chair, comparing it to the creaky old relic she sat in every day. The relic lost.

"I like Harriet. I'll bet she's a treasure."

"She's great. She was my father's secretary before he died. While I was growing up she was a real confidante, always full of 'If your dad were here now' sorts of advice." He fiddled with the papers on his desk, rearranging a heavy brass paperweight she guessed was an heirloom. "It was hard for me, growing up without him."

"Is that why you're so determined to be a father to this baby?"

"Absolutely. Even though he worked hard, my dad was always there for me, every day, in every way. I would never have been the person I am without him."

"And I would never have grown into the person I am if my parents *had* been there for me," she said simply. "For you to think you can work the long hours you do and be a father twenty-four/seven is downright foolish."

"I can try."

"And if you fail? It will be Alexis who suffers." And me, too, she added silently. "No one I know has less time than you to be a parent."

"That's what Greg says, but I'm ignoring him."

"He seems like a levelheaded guy. Maybe you should listen."

"You don't know me, Jenny, if you think I ever listen to advice after I've made up my mind."

Jenny laughed at his pompous tone. "Never confuse you with the facts, huh?"

Matt laughed, too, apparently chastened. The look in his eyes, however, signaled that he wasn't down yet.

"You've hit the nail on the head," he said, dismissing her concerns. "Now, down to business. What's the verdict? What do you think of my staff?"

"They're great people, and they love you," she admitted. "Several of them told me how honest and fair you are. They think you hung the moon."

"But are they happy?"

"Is that why you brought me here today? To find out if your people are happy? Can't you ask them?"

"They won't tell me, Jenny." He winked. "They love me."

"You are so full of it," she said, shaking her head. "I can't believe your Human Resources Department isn't keeping an eye on the needs of your employees."

"Human Resources advertises positions, hires and fires. They administer benefits and the 401K. They don't have time to worry about the little things. That's what I want to know about—improving the environment to increase output."

"You want them happier so they'll work harder?" she asked in mock outrage.

"Doesn't one thing engender the other?" he returned.

Jenny sighed. She should have known. "Yes, I guess it does."

"So, if you worked here, what would you tell me to do to make it better?"

"Okay, you asked for it," she said, slipping into her social worker role. "First, the staff meeting."

"They told you about our staff meeting?"

"Not the details," she said with a wave of her hand, dismissing his look of concern. "I don't understand enough about your business to use the information, anyway."

"All right. What about the meeting?"

"It's set for eight o'clock on Monday morning. Your staff has to come in at the crack of dawn to prepare for it. If the agenda is heavy it can last for hours."

Matt pursed his lips. She wondered if he counted himself among those who hated the marathon meetings. "Recommendation?"

"Move it to ten. Give the people a break, for heaven's sake. If it runs past noon, feed them. They're not robots, you know."

Matt grimaced, and she thought she heard him mutter *ouch*. "Serve lunch?"

"Why not? I know a great caterer. Maybe if she was over here cooking for you I wouldn't resemble a house." She patted her belly as proof.

"But lunch? Do you realize a dozen people attend that meeting?"

"Rather than let efficiency drop because they're tired and hungry, wouldn't it be better to let them eat and brainstorm solutions to the problems brought up at the meeting?"

"Well…"

"You know, Matt, since I've been pregnant I've come to realize the importance of keeping some fuel on the fire. If I get too hungry, I droop. If I snack, I can keep going like the Energizer Bunny." Almost as punctuation to her statement, her stomach growled.

Matt leaped to his feet. "Are you hungry? Why didn't you tell me? You're not going to faint or anything, are you?"

Jenny burst out laughing. She could see that Matt would be absolutely no help in a crisis. "Don't get so excited. I didn't do it on purpose."

"Hey, babe, I'm not excited. I'm just doing my job."

"Your job? What's that?"

"Taking care of my girls, of course."

For a moment Jenny's heart stopped beating. Then it pounded to a start. It almost sounded as if he cared. Cared more than just a person who wanted to snatch her baby and run.

For a moment she allowed herself to picture them as a family, standing by the crib when the baby went to sleep at night; Matt pushing a squirming, squealing Alexis in the backyard swing. She warmed to the image, closer than ever before to believing the dream. Then the vision faded, replaced by the faces of her parents, and the hope for happily ever after disappeared like smoke up the chimney on a cold winter night.

"What would you like?" Matt asked. It was a moment before she realized he was speaking of food and not her secret dreams.

"Something to drink would be fine. Juice?"

"I don't think juice is going to tame that growl, Jenny. How about a sandwich?"

Jenny nodded, resigned to letting him manage this issue by himself. He probably already knew what he wanted her to eat, anyway.

She listened as he picked up the phone and placed their order. The deli downstairs would probably make their biggest profit of the year on the array of food he ordered. She suspected some of it was destined for the staff lunch room.

Jenny was taken aback by the feeling of unease that

swept over her. The rug of her certainty was being pulled out from under her by a master.

If Matt's intention in bringing her here today was to show her what a regular guy he was, the trip had been a success. No longer just the entrepreneur who was every girl's fantasy man, he was fast becoming a real person with friends and co-workers who cared about him and ties that bound him to the community.

Unless, of course, it was all a ruse to gain her confidence and make off with her kid.

Shame on you, Jenny Ames. This was the real Matt; not some monstrous kidnapper but a person who someone not as gun-shy as Jenny would love to have in her corner.

The knowledge both scared and comforted her.

"Your snack is on its way," Matt said, interrupting her thoughts. When she looked at him she had to admit food was the last thing on her mind. Making dessert of Matt was something to be considered, though.

Jenny imagined her grandmother spinning in her grave.

"Was there anything else on your list?"

"Actually, yes. I think you should consider establishing some kind of in-house day care program. It would improve efficiency if the moms and dads who worked for you didn't have to worry about their kids during the day."

"That sounds expensive."

Jenny smiled. Poor Matt. Poor Matt's wallet. "Not when you consider the drop in absenteeism that would result."

"You've got this all figured out, haven't you?"

"Maybe. When it comes to services for women and children, my mind tends to work pretty fast."

Within seconds she could tell his mind was working, too. His eyes narrowed, but she saw that his frown was spoiled by the tiniest smile tipping the corner of his mouth.

"I'm not promising anything, okay?" he said gruffly.

"Okay," Jenny agreed, but she could see in his eyes that it was a done deal.

The trip to Hope's House had been a success. She'd suspected there was compassion in him. Now she knew.

A feeling of accomplishment curled warmly into her stomach. She felt like twirling her pistols on her fingertips and blowing away the smoke with a puff of air from lips that wouldn't stop smiling.

"What are you going to do about child care when Alexis is born?" he asked after they were seated with their meal from the deli. Phrased so nonchalantly, the question put Jenny on alert.

"I'll be working from home for the first six weeks or so," she said cautiously. "Then I'll take a portable crib to the office."

He popped the tab on a soda and offered it to her. She declined with a shake of her head.

"What if you have to go out to meetings?"

"I'll hire a sitter. Some of the neighborhood grandmas have already offered."

"Would you consider dropping her off here?"

"No."

He frowned. She could see him puffing up for a fight. "Did you ever consider that I'd like to have a say in the day care arrangements?"

"No."

"Why not?"

Jenny thought a minute before answering, then considered it only fair to tell the truth. Resigned, she shrugged. "I thought you'd be gone by now."

"Think again, Jenny." He flipped his sandwich over to unwrap it, nearly crushing it with hands that clenched in anger. "Think again."

Chapter Nine

"I wish you wouldn't look at me that way." Jenny wiped her mouth and returned her napkin to her lap. It had taken only minutes for her to decimate the sandwich Matt provided.

"What way? It's no secret that I find you very beautiful."

She snorted, an impatient, indelicate sound, rude and derisive. What was going on with her? It seemed that once she got tanked up on fruit juice and deli turkey the urge to pick a fight was too strong to ignore.

Matt had unwittingly put her back against the wall with his arguments about Alexis's care. Her opinion of him was changing; she couldn't deny that. But the idea of letting him take Lexie, even for a short period of time, terrified her. She fidgeted, then leaped to her feet, ready to fight. "That's the way you looked at *her,*" she said angrily.

"What the devil are you talking about?"

"Krystal. At the party. I saw the two of you, you know. She was all over you and you loved every minute of it."

"For your information, Miss Jump-to-Conclusions," Matt said with undisguised sarcasm, "I told her to get lost."

"Well, she still wants you, that was obvious."

"But I don't want her."

"She said—"

"Ah, now we get to the meat of the matter. What exactly did Krystal say to you? *Exactly.*"

"She said you were drawn to her like a moth to a flame." She said it airily, like she didn't care, although she did.

Matt pursed his lips. "Go on."

"She said that sooner or later you'd find proof the baby is yours."

"And?"

Suddenly the fight went out of her, like a balloon that lost its air. "I'm sorry. I shouldn't have said anything."

"What did she say?"

Jenny closed her eyes to squeeze back the tears. "That you would take Lexie away from me," she whispered.

Matt rose and walked to her. Taking her chin in his hand, he turned her face to his. "Look at me."

When she opened her eyes, the tears she'd tried so valiantly to hold back rained down her cheeks. He used his thumbs to sweep them away.

"Is this why you've been running? Trying to scare me off?"

"I didn't know what else to do. You and I are too different. You make me feel as if I don't have any choices about my own life anymore. I don't want to hurt you, but I don't think I can give you what you want."

"I'm not going to take your baby away from you. Do you understand me?" He rested his hands on her shoulders. "But that doesn't mean I don't want to know if she's mine. You can't continue to deny me the knowledge of my own child."

"I know that. I don't mean to be unfair." She took a shuddering breath and let go of some of the fear. "I'll let the hospital do the blood tests when Lexie's born."

"Thank you." He briefly touched Jenny's cheek with trembling fingers, then kissed her gently. "I know I can get a little carried away when there's something I want, but I promise I'll never hurt you intentionally."

"I want to believe that, but you don't really know me."

"There isn't anything you could tell me that would make me think any less of you."

She looked at him, evaluating his mysterious remark, doing her best to make him feel like a bug under a magnifying glass. She crossed her arms over her breasts and glared at him the way her grandmothers had so often done.

"You know about Australia, don't you."

He nodded, but she could tell how reluctant he was to admit intruding in her life.

"I thought so. One of the neighbors said there was a strange man asking questions about me. It was shortly after we met, so I assumed you were behind it. She called the authorities, you know."

Matt groaned. "We won't be using that investigator again."

"The police sent a detective out to talk to me, but I told him not to worry. It was very embarrassing. Cops are not stupid people."

"Thank you for keeping my secret."

"What secret? That sometimes you act like an idiot?"

Matt laughed wryly. "Something like that." His voice softened. "Did he hurt you?"

"Do you mean, did he rape me?" Jenny turned and walked slowly to the window. She stood, looking out at the river, and hugged her belly in a protective gesture.

"No, he didn't." Behind her, Matt let out the breath he'd been holding. That seemed to be his only reaction.

"I had some bruises on my arms, and on my breast where he grabbed me. I was very badly frightened."

She remembered him, the monster who'd left her with her virginity but had taken away her innocence. He'd smelled of sweat and stale beer and seemed to think her parents had sent her there for his amusement. "When I screamed and fought he tore my blouse and dragged me toward his bedroom."

She shuddered, lost in a memory that brought her both shame and pride. "I swung my arm around as hard as I could and managed to break his jaw. He let me go, and I ran into the bush. Would you believe it? My dad took that jerk to the hospital before he came to look for me. I guess he thought a night in the wilderness would subdue me, but it only fueled my anger. Just for spite, I waited until they called in the police before I came out."

"Good for you."

"Actually, the worst part came later. My parents blamed me for what happened. When they left me at the airport they didn't say goodbye or even tell me if I'd see them again."

She removed her hands from her belly and let them drop to her sides.

"This is weird. It's the first time I've talked about it to anyone other than police and social workers. My grandmother…well, the less said about her the better. Suffice it to say, she acted like it never happened, like it was too dirty to discuss." She looked Matt directly in the eye and clenched her teeth when she spoke. "I can't begin to tell you how angry that made me."

"Why didn't you tell me about it?"

She laughed roughly. "You mean aside from the fact that it's none of your business?"

"Yeah." He shrugged, but there was something in his voice that was both apologetic and encouraging. "Aside from that."

"It's not something I like to talk about. 'Hi, my name is Jenny and I was molested when I was sixteen.' Too much of an ice-breaker, if you ask me."

"That's not funny," he said tersely. She could see his fists were clenched; his shoulders stiffened with anger.

She sighed. "I didn't tell you before because I was afraid you'd use it to take the baby away from me. It wouldn't be the first time a man used a woman's past to hurt her. Let me tell you something, Matt Hanson. What happened was not my fault. I didn't do anything wrong."

"I never thought you did.

"My mother sent me over there," she said in a voice rising with emotion, "with some film of a dive they'd made in the Great Barrier Reef. He pulled me inside, damn it, I didn't go willingly."

"I know, honey. You were young and couldn't possibly have known the dangers you were facing. I think you're very brave and very honest."

"But I'm still standing in the way of what you want."

"You don't have any idea what I want. If your concerns about my intentions are what's keeping us from being friends—then, I'm sorry. I want to help you if I can, protect you and the baby if you need it."

"I appreciate the thought, but that won't be necessary. I'm all the protection my baby needs." Her voice turned cold. "If anyone ever tries to hurt Alexis, I'll kill them with my bare hands."

Matt stepped forward and took Jenny in his arms and rested his lips near her ear. "My sweetheart," he whispered. "My little warrior. I promise you this. If anyone ever tries to hurt Alexis, I'll help you."

Jenny turned her head toward Matt's chest and let her cheek rest on the soft wool of his jacket. She hadn't thought he'd be so kind. How could he have known the right words to say to help her feel not so alone? In all her life, no one had ever been there for her the way he was today. She didn't even know how to thank him. It was so great a gift she couldn't begin to imagine how to repay it.

Sitting back on the windowsill, Matt drew her toward him so that she stood between his knees. He took her hands in his, pressing them to his chest. Involuntarily her fingers curled around his.

When he finally captured her gaze with his, the eyes that had captured her heart were liquid with tenderness. The iron carapace around her heart cracked a little with the knowledge that he might, possibly, be as unsure as she was.

With her fingers resting against his chest she was aware, as never before, of the swift pace of his heart. It beat quickly, like Lexie's when the doctor let her listen to the Doppler amplifier in his office.

His thighs, where they pressed against her legs, were taut, but not confining. Strong, but not oppressive. She was tempted to let down her guard…tempted, but not convinced it was the right thing to do just yet. As if he sensed her imminent flight, Matt spoke slowly, his voice soft and seductive, like his touch…like his kisses.

"We haven't known each other for very long, but there's something between us…something special."

Jenny grew impatient. They'd been down this road before. "Don't say that, Matt—"

"Hear me out, okay?" His hands tightened over hers. "I'm a careful and cautious kind of guy. One who never makes decisions without a lot of thought. When I found out about the baby I went kind of crazy. I had certain plans in place for my life and within the space of a day or two the whole world went spinning off its axis."

Matt frowned and bit his lip. "I took a lot of pleasure in scaring you half to death that day in your office, and I've beaten myself up for it more than once since."

"I understand how you felt…maybe not then, but I do now. You don't have to—"

"Did I tell you why I broke up with Krystal?" he asked suddenly. She recognized the pain in his eyes, but to her relief, no regret. She knew he didn't love the beautiful model anymore, but his pain was almost more than Jenny could bear. Tears pricked the backs of her eyes and choked her throat. She wanted to speak, but the words wouldn't come.

She shook her head.

"She told me she was afraid of getting pregnant because it would affect her bookings. I could understand how she felt. She'd worked as hard building her career as I had on my business. I wanted to be fair. We agreed I would do the sperm donation and then I'd get a vasectomy."

Jenny gasped.

"Krystal was afraid of an accident. On the day of the surgery I changed my mind. When I went to her house to break the news, I overheard her telling a friend she'd tricked me into having the surgery, and that she really only wanted my money."

"I'm so sorry."

"No, don't be. Don't you see? That's what brought us together. I can't be sorry about anything that resulted in you being pregnant with my child."

Jenny stiffened with anger. Didn't he understand that she wanted him to want her, too, not just the baby inside her?

"But it's not just the baby," he said quickly. She swore he'd read her mind. "I'm so happy to have met you, to be able to get to know you and what's important to you. I'm beginning to discover ways I can be of some use to the world, ways to make the time I've spent making money have purpose. Each day I'm more content than I was the day before."

"I'm happy for you, Matt, but I think you would have found your way into the real world eventually. No one can stay hidden behind glass walls and iron gates forever, you know."

"I know, but I'm glad you're my guide."

His eyes left hers and dropped to her belly. He scanned her body from breasts to thighs, igniting a fever that sent her emotions streaking up into the stratosphere.

The room was quiet with just the sounds of their breathing to break the silence…his deep and rough, hers shallow and tremulous. The tension between them was palpable. Jenny knew she should step back to break the spell, but couldn't. Whether it was fear or curiosity that held her there, she didn't know. Each time Matt looked at her, a little more of her resistance melted away. His eyes were like fingers. They caressed her body, arousing her, making up for the sex they hadn't had in order to create their child.

He watched her every movement, measured her every breath, pushing her temperature, her desire, higher. Each flicker of interest in his eyes, each grin, each turn of his head made it seem as though he were listening for a message from inside her.

She'd had so many minutes of this communion time with the baby she couldn't deny him his turn. He released her hands and reached toward her.

"Can I see her?"

She caught his hand in midair and brought it to her belly. The warmth of his skin permeated her sweater and the light fabric of her leggings. It felt so good, she couldn't resist.

Her head sent out warnings, *Mayday, mayday, heart in jeopardy,* but she ignored them all. The last thing on her mind was being sensible.

Matt pushed her sweater upward and eased her waistband down, baring her to his gaze. His sharp intake of breath made her catch her own. Did he find her ugly? It certainly wasn't the taut, flat stomach of a supermodel.

He looked up at her, awe and amazement in his eyes. "So beautiful." He rested his hands against her skin, his fingers spread wide. Predictably, Lexie shifted, a long, lazy movement from one side of Jenny's abdomen to the other. "It really is a miracle."

He rubbed his hands seductively over her skin. His thumb toyed with her protruding navel. "Have you always been an outie, Jen?"

Matt leaned forward and kissed Jenny's belly, reinforcing her own belief in the incredible magic of life. She laughed and rested her hands on his head in an effort to hold him to her for a moment longer.

There was one miracle yet to make an appearance in Jenny's life. Matt's fascination with the baby inside her was one manifestation of love, but that didn't mean he could, or ever would, fall in love with her.

Damn. When would it ever be her turn?

Tears rushed to her eyes, and she stepped back abruptly.

"I'm sorry, Matt. I can't…" She pulled her sweater down roughly and he had to pull his hands back to keep them from getting trapped by the flurry of soft wool and trembling hands. He stood, but she eluded him. She raced to the chair by Matt's desk and grabbed her purse, looking frantically for an escape route. Matt, confusion apparent on his face, pointed to the door of a small powder room at the rear of the large office. Jenny rushed, or rather, waddled, toward it, her face turned away to hide her embarrassment.

Jenny slipped into the ladies' room, leaving Matt to his muddled thoughts. What the heck happened? Touching her had been one of the most beautiful, meaningful events of his life, but apparently Jenny didn't agree. At first she had welcomed his touch, but then something, he might never know what, changed.

If she would only talk to him about her fears, he might be able to assuage them. And if she wouldn't… well, he was definitely going to have to consider padding the walls of his office, because Jenny was going to drive him crazy for sure.

The insistent ringing of a telephone drew him from

his thoughts. The sound was coming from Jenny's brief-case. He fished out the phone. Knowing how long wom-en could take in the bathroom, he figured she'd be another hour, at least.

"Matt?" Nancy asked when he answered the phone. "Where's Jenny? Is she all right?"

"She's fine, Nancy. She's a bit indisposed at the mo-ment. May I help you?"

"Could you give her a message for me? My parents are coming home early from a business trip and I need to meet them at the airport. I was supposed to go to Lamaze class with her tonight, but I'm going to have to cancel."

"You're her labor coach?"

"Yes."

"Why didn't she ask me?"

"Probably because she didn't know you when she signed up."

"When did classes start?"

"Last week was the first one."

"Then it's not too late for me to catch up."

"Oh, Lord," she groaned. "She'd going to hammer me for telling you about this."

"Don't worry. I'll defend you."

"I was kidding. She's not the type to hold grudges. Once a friend, always a friend in Jenny's world."

"That's good to know. I'll give her the message." He grinned. He owed Nancy big-time for this one.

The bathroom door opened and Jenny emerged, fif-ty-five minutes ahead of schedule, at least.

"Did I hear the phone? I told Nancy to call if she needed me."

"Good guess. She asked me to tell you she can't go to Lamaze with you tonight."

"Uh-oh." She reached out and took her briefcase from him, holding it in front of her like a shield.

"When were you going to tell me?"

"I thought I might show you my certificate of completion."

"That's generous of you. Where are you having the baby?"

"University." Matt grimaced and Jenny could almost see him thinking, *A public hospital?* As if she wanted to deliver in some high-priced day spa where they probably wouldn't let her see her baby without an appointment.

"Who's your doctor now?"

"I don't have one yet."

"What do you mean you don't have one yet?

"I've been looking," she protested. "I can't seem to find anyone who's willing to take me on this late in the game."

"That's ridiculous. Who have you called?"

"Every doctor on my insurance plan list."

"Did you call Dan Wilson?"

"The most famous OB-GYN in Ohio? Are you kidding? I couldn't afford him in a million years."

"I can. Besides, he's my neighbor and I'm sure he owes me at least one favor. I'll talk to him this afternoon and let you know what he says when I pick you up."

"Pick me up?"

"For Lamaze. Surely you don't think now that I know about the class I'm not going with you. Jeez, Jenny. You know me better than that."

"Bad idea."

"Why?" Suspicion clouded his eyes, and Jenny was on the spot again.

Dropping the briefcase back on the chair, she clasped

her hands before her. Her eyebrows knotted in consternation. "Childbirth preparation is very, um, physical. You'd have to, well, touch me and I'd have to, sort of, lean on you and let you hold me."

"Like we just did?"

Jenny's mouth made a little *O,* and he resisted the urge to kiss it away.

"You think I'm not up to it?" he asked with a grin. He lifted his arm, bent it at the elbow and flexed it like a body builder. "Here, feel my muscle."

Instead of doing as he asked, she linked her hands behind her. She'd been touching him, and he touching her, *way* too much lately.

It was wonderful.

It had to stop.

Jenny was beginning to think there was something wrong with her brain. Matt was handsome, intelligent and as thoughtful as a man could be. He was strong and gentle. Why couldn't she trust him?

He'd admitted he got carried away when he wanted something. Where would it stop? Why wouldn't he back off and let her be? How was she supposed to decide what to do with him standing so close, taking up all the oxygen she needed to think?

Yet there he stood, fidgeting, waiting for her to make up what remained of her mind.

He had the oddest look in his eyes. Before Jenny could react, or rather, run, he reached out and slipped his arms around her. She froze.

He leaned forward and took her mouth in a kiss meant to erase all doubt. Not at all like the lazy, searching kiss they'd shared on the elevator, this one demanded a response, and Jenny knew the response he wanted was yes. Yes, you can have anything you want, Matt. Yes, you'll get your way.

"I'm up to the challenge, Jenny, I swear it."

She felt the blood rush to her cheeks. "You know what I mean," she whispered.

Matt moved closer until his taut belly met her very rounded one. He leaned forward to whisper in her ear.

"Am I not good at giving back rubs?" he asked, his voice low. It sent shivers up and down her spine.

"And when we were on the elevator and you leaned into me, I did that right, too, didn't I?"

"But that was just us. There are other people, other couples—" married couples, she thought "—in the class."

He seemed to read her uneasiness and stepped back for a moment. He reached out to touch her cheek. Even though she wished he wouldn't, she couldn't bring herself to ask him to stop.

"Tell you what," he said slowly. "I'll ask Steadman to take you home so you can rest. I'll come over later and you can let me know whether it's a go or no for Lamaze, okay?"

Jenny shook her head uncertainly.

"Think about it, okay?"

"I will," she said, feeling the fight go out of her.

And she would, too. No more going on emotion and mind-numbing kisses and tender touches instead of reason and cold hard facts. No more roller-coaster rides between fear and suspicion and trust and…and…damn it.

Just because a man always said the right thing didn't mean he was Mr. Right.

Just because it seemed he could read your mind, or knew what you wanted or needed almost before you did, didn't mean he did it for any reason other than ego or duty.

Just because you fell in love with him didn't mean he would fall in love with you. Ever.

Chapter Ten

"Whoa, little girl." Jenny laughed as she rubbed her belly with both hands and resumed her motion on the front porch swing. "Let's save the tae kwon do lessons for after you're born, okay?"

She'd spent what was left of the unusually balmy fall afternoon sitting on the porch, rocking and talking to Alexis about her troublesome father. Since Lexie rarely held up her end of a conversation, Jenny found herself talking to herself a lot.

"You know, Lex, I think we're doing all right on our own. Your daddy has been very nice to us—I won't say it hasn't been fun riding around in that big limo—but to tell you the truth, I'm beginning to feel a little hemmed in."

Jenny paused in her swinging to listen for some protest from within. There was only silence.

She used her foot to push off from the smooth wood

floor of the porch. The lazy back and forth of the swing relaxed her, but she knew the effect was only temporary. She'd complained she needed space to think, so what did she do when Matt sent her home, alone, to think to her heart's content?

She thought about him.

She sighed and allowed her mouth to droop, her mind and heart a muddle of conflicting emotions.

Matt believed he could have anything he wanted if he was willing to work for it, and apparently what he wanted now was to be a part-time father to Lexie.

In Jenny's experience, family—the father/mother/carefree-child kind—was a phantom. Fathers left, or let you down. Those who remained lived their disappointment and disillusionment on a daily basis.

Her proof lay at her side on the swing. She'd dug out the old family album, and her conviction was strengthened with each page she turned. Here were her grandmothers in their wedding finery, smiling for photographers, hope shining in their eyes. In later years they were portrayed alone, bitterness pinching from their faces whatever happiness might have remained.

Then came the pictures of her parents smiling broadly for the camera at the church, then on their honeymoon on some sun-drenched island. Most hurtful was the one of her mother pregnant, her father's hand resting on her mother's belly, forced smiles on their faces.

The remaining photos in the book were of Jenny: first grade, second grade and on and on until her graduation from college. Her great-grandmother had died shortly thereafter and Jenny began keeping her own album. It reflected a family of one, except for the most recent photo, taken by Nancy at the party only a few days before.

Lexie would see it someday and know she was a wanted child.

That, however, could never change the fact that Matt's participation in her conception had been an accident. Sure, he was all gung-ho about the baby now, but what would happen when she went from fetus to reality?

It was easy for Matt to send out chauffeurs and caterers, to call the deli for sandwiches, but who would take care of the 2:00 a.m. feedings and runny noses?

Jenny would.

She felt like a piece of rope in a game of tug-of-war. Apprehension stood tugging on one side, longing on the other. She wanted Matt and the security he represented, but the minute she decided to set aside her fears and enjoy the pleasures he offered, some unpleasant memory would come back to haunt her. The past always made sure she knew that loneliness and disappointment were right around the bend.

If she told Matt to beat it, he might sue for custody. That fear was enough to stop her from breaking off the relationship with him. Yet the longer she let him hang around, the more her heart was in jeopardy.

How did a person learn to trust?

Letting her head fall back, Jenny breathed deeply. A burst of wind, cool and sharp, stirred leaves in the yard next to the porch. A single leaf fluttered to rest atop the photo album.

It all went back to the parent thing.

Matt revered his father. He wanted to be like him, wanted his life to be a tribute to the man's short years as a dad. In all their conversations he'd never mentioned his mother, but Jenny would bet she was a saint, whether living or not.

Jenny, on the other hand, hated her parents. Well, maybe *hated* was too strong a word, but she certainly had no great love for them, and absolutely zero admiration for their parenting skills.

She was determined they would never know Alexis. That would be their punishment; it was the worst one Jenny could think of. The most beautiful, gifted, generous spirit ever to grace the earth would be their granddaughter, and if Jenny had her way, they would never lay eyes on her. Never in a million years.

No doubt a bunch of psychiatrists would have a field day with that little pledge, but sometimes you had to call a spade a spade and get on with your life as best you could.

Which brought her back to Matt Hanson.

Which, coincidentally, brought Matt to her house. She heard him before she actually saw him, the engine of a huge SUV roaring as he pulled up in front of the house. It had grown late, and the last rays of the sun glinted off the silver Cadillac nameplate.

Draperies and blinds flickered up and down the usually quiet street. Neighbors, the caring and the curious, peered out to see the noisy visitor.

Matt hopped out of the vehicle, his tight jeans and cable-knit sweater carelessly topped by a soft leather jacket. Desire pooled low in Jenny's belly, then loosened and spiraled out to the tips of her toes and fingers. Her heart raced a little.

Alexis gave her a sharp kick, as if to say, "Hey, Mom. It's just Dad."

And Alexis was right. It was just Matt.

He would stay, or he would go.

There wasn't a thing she could do about it either way, regardless of what her heart wanted. He wasn't a monster, she conceded with relief. He was generous and easy on the eyes.

So why not enjoy it while it lasted?

Jenny smiled and waved a greeting. From a distance she saw Matt's dark eyes widen with surprise.

He jogged up the sidewalk then bounced on the balls of his feet up to the porch. It was the most physical thing she'd ever seen him do, but it made sense. Athletic baby, athletic daddy.

He took up a position by the railing, feet crossed, hands thrust deep into the pockets of his jacket.

He didn't kiss her. He didn't rush up to her and take her into his arms for one of his patented bear hugs. He didn't ask how his girls were.

He didn't have any idea how disappointed Jenny was.

How exactly was she supposed to enjoy whatever lasted as long as it lasted if he wasn't going to go along with the plan?

Trust Matt to scramble things up.

Again.

"Hi," she said. "Where's Mr. Steadman?"

"I gave him the night off," Matt responded. "How are you doing? Did you rest?"

"Nope. Too much action from the cheap seats," she said, patting her belly.

"More ballet?"

"More like kickboxing. At least she'll get a sports scholarship to college and save me some money."

"I'll take care of her expenses, Jenny."

"No need. I started a college fund when I got pregnant."

Matt dropped his head and seemed to find the toes of his shoes incredibly interesting. Jenny thought she detected a slight blush across his high cheekbones and wondered if he'd found out about the savings account the same way he'd learned about her misadventures down under.

"Is there anything you don't know about me?" she asked.

He looked up, obviously embarrassed at having been caught in a further deception. "Can we talk about this later?"

"We don't have to talk about it at all. I'm not upset."

"You're not?" He was genuinely surprised.

She shook her head. "What's done is done. You were protecting yourself. I probably would have done the same if I'd had the money. Besides, Nancy told me a little about you, and I figured if you had any bad habits I would have read about them in the *Inquirer* by now."

"*Cincinnati* or *National?*" he asked with a laugh.

"Both," she countered with a smile.

He levered his body away from the railing and walked to the end of the porch. Looking out at the leaf-strewn yard he sighed, then turned back to Jenny.

"So what's the verdict?"

"Verdict?" she asked, puzzled.

"The Lamaze class."

"What do you think? As if I could keep you from doing whatever you want to do."

"That sounds like a yes."

"I guess so. Even if it turns out you're not my labor coach, I still need the practice. I'm warning you, though. This is not your traditional Lamaze class. It's sort of New Age. Long on relaxation techniques and short on the gory details."

"That's fine with me. Whatever you can dish out, I can take. Let's go."

"Class isn't for a couple of hours."

"I thought we could stop for something to eat."

"I ate at your office."

Matt checked his shiny Rolex. Jenny rolled her eyes.

"It's been three hours and forty-seven minutes since you ate," he said. "Gotta keep fuel on that fire, don't we?"

Jenny's eyes stopped in midroll and narrowed suspiciously. "You keep track of stuff like that? You need to get a life, Matt."

"I have a life and I like it fine, Jenny. All it lacks is a basic knowledge of the Lamaze method of childbirth."

Jenny settled back and pushed the swing into motion with her foot. "I've been thinking—"

"I've been thinking, too, and I'm not crazy about the way things have been going between us. Ever since we met I've done nothing but argue and hurt your feelings. I've even made you cry. But we've never done anything for fun."

"I had fun with you in the elevator today." She grinned, trying to lessen the seriousness of the conversation.

"We can't spend all our time kissing."

"No?" She tried, and failed, to keep the disappointment out of her voice.

"Not that it wouldn't be pleasant," he conceded with a grin. "Now that I think about it, it's a damn good idea."

As he walked toward her he studied her openly, his bold gaze raking her from the sloppy bun on the top of her head to the toes of her nonskid shoes. It was like being touched, slowly and tenderly, by a lover.

"You were wonderful," he said, his voice low. His eyes made their way back up her body to her lips. "Your mouth tasted like honey and you were soft and so sweet in my arms." He shook his head and exhaled roughly. "You made me ache in the damnedest places."

Jenny's hopes leaped, knowing that their closeness affected him as it did her. Her pulse thundered, her thoughts grew fuzzy.

Matt dropped to one knee in front of her. For one heart-stopping moment she thought he might propose. He rested his hands on her thighs but made no attempt to touch her belly or make contact with the baby in any way. The swing stopped and their eyes met. The sharp pain of longing tore through her body, and she shivered.

"I'd made my mind up not to touch you tonight, but being with you makes me lose all my good sense. I scared you this afternoon, didn't I?"

She started to shake her head, to protest, but he stopped her with a whispered word.

"Don't. I saw the fear in your eyes. You try hard to hide your feelings from me, but tonight your face is so expressive; your eyes reveal every truth."

She prayed he was wrong. If the desires of her soul were reflected in her eyes, the game would be up.

Matt took her hands and stood, grinning, breaking the tension that hung around them like a shroud.

"Do me a favor?"

Jenny gave him the best smile she could muster. "Sure."

"I know this lady who's going to have a baby. As her friend, I'd like to be as much help as I can. I was thinking that if I knew something about prepared childbirth, like breathing or relaxation, it might come in handy."

She nodded. "It might."

"Well, I heard by way of the grapevine, the Nancy-vine, I think it was, that you've got a Lamaze class tonight."

"That's true."

He drew her up next to him. "I was wondering if you'd let me tag along and see if I could learn anything. No strings attached, of course."

Her heart broke a little when she answered.

"No strings, Matt. No strings at all."

Jenny woke to warmth and quiet. She didn't remember her pillow ever being this firm and unyielding nor her bed this hard. She leaned back and tried to snuggle in, but the surface upon which she rested refused to give.

"Sweetheart?" her pillow asked, and then rumbled jovially beneath her. "C'mon honey, it's time to wake up."

Jenny struggled to rouse from her dream, in which she was a tiny baby being held by an uncommonly handsome man who resembled Matt. Her eyelids fluttered, then opened. Before her lay the silent, empty auditorium. When her head lolled to the side, she saw the Lamaze coach seated tailor-style beside her, grinning from ear to ear.

Behind her, Matt rocked slowly, easing her into wakefulness. His arms were the arms of her dreams.

The final exercise of the night taught relaxation during labor. Like the other labor coaches, Matt had sat behind her, supporting her on either side with his muscled, jeans-clad legs. She'd rested her hands on his forearms while his fingers made lazy circles on her belly. The lights were low. Mozart played on the stereo.

And she'd fallen asleep.

Heaven help her, she'd let her head drop back on Matt's broad shoulder and she'd fallen into so deep a sleep that she hadn't even awakened when the class was dismissed.

Never in her entire life had she been so embarrassed, unless she counted the time in Matt's car.

Oh, why not? That made two, *two* times she'd been so embarrassed she lost the power of speech, so humiliated she couldn't even look him in the eye.

Matt helped Jenny to her feet while the instructor chattered on about the "little mamas" who fell asleep during her class. Matt seemed to find it amusing, but Jenny certainly wasn't prepared to give the woman any ribbons for her ability to put embarrassed people at ease.

Matt guided her to the car, his hand at the small of her back. She was so aware of his presence she could barely put one foot in front of the other without stumbling. He didn't seem to notice, though.

As they drove through the night, he occasionally pointed out some landmark and told how it related to his childhood. Jenny laughed out loud when she realized she'd played softball on the same lot as he, although she was willing to bet he hadn't gotten a stern lecture when he got home because his lace-trimmed anklets were dusty.

Jenny realized, quite against her will, that Matt was a regular guy who just happened to grow up to be absolutely extraordinary. That boded well for Alexis, who would most likely grow up to be extraordinary, too.

"You're quiet," Matt said as he pulled up to a light.

"I'm usually quiet like this when I think."

"What are you thinking about?"

"The usual stuff."

"What kind of stuff?"

"Work things. Baby things. House things."

"Any 'things' I can help with?" His look was hopeful.

"No, thanks." She breathed a sigh of relief when he

didn't protest, but merely turned his attention back to the road.

The traffic light changed to green. Matt put on his left-turn indicator and glanced at her, saying, "You're thinking too hard. I know where to go to cure what ails you."

"What? Where? My house is the other way."

"Wait and see. You trust me, don't you? You trusted me enough this evening to fall asleep in my arms—"

"Matt," she said in a warning tone.

"And don't think I didn't appreciate it, uh...your show of trust, I mean. But now I think I've got an idea you're gonna like."

"What?" She couldn't keep the tone of suspicion from her voice.

He reached over and squeezed her hand.

"Just wait. You'll see."

Of all the things that epitomized Cincinnati, Graeter's ice cream was his favorite. Sitting in the old-timey parlor watching Jenny eat a raspberry chocolate cone was definitely high on the list of the highlights of his life. Everyone around them seemed to notice, too, and it made him smile, because she was with him tonight, was *his,* at least tonight.

Jenny's tongue emerged from between her lips and slid up the side of the huge dollops of ice cream. Matt imagined her tongue, slow and languid, on a particular part of his body. That part, tightly encased in blue denim, responded in a manner most painful. Matt groaned, eliciting a sharp look from Jenny. He swallowed, then choked out, "Yum."

"Look out, Lexie," Jenny said, almost to herself.

"Here comes one of the greatest pleasures known to womankind."

Matt's eyes nearly popped out of his head. She couldn't possibly be imagining the same pleasures as he. The thought of Jenny, naked beside him in a cozy bed, her fair hair spread out across a satin pillow, her moist, well-kissed lips parted in anticipation of more...well, ice cream it wasn't.

When he managed to refocus his gaze he found her watching him. Her eyes were large and liquid, darkening to the amethyst he knew signaled her thoughts, almost as if she'd read his mind. If ever there was a woman ripe for kissing—lots of kissing—it was Jenny Ames.

She blinked and swayed as she sat before him, as though she were light headed. As though she'd read both his mind and his intent. His hand cupped the back of her head, anchoring her.

"You know," he said thoughtfully, continuing to hold her gaze. "I bet if I kissed you right now you'd taste like raspberries and chocolate."

"Want to experiment?" she asked. There was a challenge in her eyes he hadn't seen before. She was toying with him and he liked it.

Really liked it.

"I'm game if you are," she continued, showing him her siren's smile. "I mean, it's not the elevator at your office, but we could make do."

Matt leaned forward, peering into her eyes. "Is that you in there, Jenny? I'm beginning to think you've been abducted by aliens and replaced by a vamp."

She laughed, that same light innocent kind of laugh that always made his body go crazy, and he knew she was back, with both feet planted firmly on good old Ohio soil.

"Why don't we save the experimenting for later. It looks like we have an audience here."

"Oops," she said, eyeing the crowd at the counter. "Darn that sugar rush." She crossed her eyes comically.

"I think we need to keep you away from sweets," Matt said as he led her to the car.

On the way back to her house Jenny's expectations blossomed. He hadn't wanted to kiss her at the ice cream parlor—no, actually that wasn't true. She'd have bet her last dime he *had* wanted to kiss her, but being the no-public-displays-of-affection kind of guy he was, she knew why he wanted to wait.

She was betting he'd be hell on wheels in the glow of the porch light.

When they pulled up in front of the house, she waited for him to help her down from the truck's high seat. He walked her to the porch, again resting his hand at the small of her back as if he were her rudder. Taking her small purse from her hands, he fished for the key, unlocked the door and then returned both items to her.

"Did you have a good time tonight?"

"Sure. Anytime I get ice cream, a nap and a few laughs out of the deal I consider myself a winner."

"Cute." He zipped his jacket and flipped up the collar against the chilly night air.

Jenny watched his every move, wondering if he'd changed his mind and would simply say good-night and leave. Disappointment settled in around her heart, then fled as he reached forward, took her in his arms and rested his mouth firmly against hers.

She thought she knew Matt's kisses, but she was

mistaken. Tonight, along with the tenderness, there was a hint of desperation in his touch. He kissed her slowly, drawing back, then pressing forward to outline the fullness of her lips with his tongue, tasting her as if she were the perfect confection, even better than the ice cream they'd so recently eaten.

She kept asking herself what it meant, this urgency. It seemed fruitless to wonder, so she simply let her mind go blank, became nothing but feelings and sensation.

Raising his head, he gazed into her eyes. Like so many times before she found herself drowning in warm chocolate.

"Can I come in?"

Jenny shook her head "No."

He closed in on her again, tenderness replacing insistence. His lips were more persuasive than she would ever admit, even to herself. But her resolve was not shaken.

If she let him in she'd never get the memories out of her house. Or out of her heart.

"You make me hungry. So hungry. I don't think I could ever get enough of you."

Another kiss, this one whisper soft, on her lips. Then others on her closed eyelids and on her cheek, then her jaw, and then a trail of kisses down her neck.

"Come home with me."

"Why?"

"Because I want you."

"No, Matt. That's too big a step for me. I won't deny that I like kissing you, but my feelings are too unsettled for anything more."

He closed his eyes and sighed. "I wasn't going to touch you tonight. I was going to wait and let you come to me." His eyes opened. They burned with a purposeful inner fire. "I guess you're not ready. I guess the question is whether or not you'll ever be ready."

Rather than apologize, she remained silent. What could she say that she hadn't said already?

Matt backed up, taking the warmth with him. She snuggled into her cape.

"I forgot to tell you," he said, his voice devoid of emotion. "You have an appointment with Daniel Wilson at eight o'clock in the morning. Will you see him? We'll pick you up at seven-thirty."

"I'll be ready."

He stepped forward again, although this time he didn't touch her except to drop a soft kiss on her forehead.

"Go in," he said roughly.

"Till morning, then," she whispered, and slipped inside.

Matt climbed into his truck. Instead of starting the engine he rested his head on the steering wheel. His body was as tight as a bowstring for the second time that day. What was it this woman did to him that made him feel like an untried teenager?

"I wish you were here with me, Dad," he said to the night. "I could use some of your advice."

Anything worth having is worth waiting for, Matt.

He heard the words in his heart as well as in his head. Except for dying so young, his father had never let him down. Matt felt the presence, the love, of the man he admired more than any other.

"I feel like time's running out. What if I do, or say, the wrong thing and lose them?"

Follow your heart. You'll never go wrong if you follow your heart.

He'd forgotten that one. How many times had his father admonished him to look inside himself for the answers he needed? Although he'd been too young for advice about girls, before his father passed away they'd talked at length about growing up. Being a man. The lessons he'd learned from his dad and the social conventions pounded into his head by his mom hadn't let him down yet.

He'd dated women more beautiful than Jenny, but none of them were more attractive to him than she was. Hell, Krystal was touted in fashion magazines as one of the most exquisite women in the world. Yet, looking back, he realized that even though he'd wanted her sexually he'd never sought any kind of emotional union with her. He wondered why he'd ever thought he wanted to marry and have children with her. Must've been his hormones.

Or maybe he'd simply grown up.

With Jenny it was different; everything was different. She had a beauty that glowed from within; it wasn't painted on. She liked people and cared about them. She wanted children and wasn't worried about the extra pounds or the stretch marks.

And she could kiss like a house on fire.

With Krystal, he'd always looked forward to the nights.

With Jenny, he thought about the future.

Chapter Eleven

Awe.

Matt found himself completely in awe of his small daughter; amazed by her tiny fingers and toes, her rounded knees, the perfectly formed eyes gazing at him from a small video monitor. If ever there was a sight worthy of jumbo-tron, this was it.

Dan Wilson stood behind him, clearly amused.

"I take it this is the first time you've seen a 4-D sonogram," he commented.

"This is the first time I've seen any kind of sonogram. It's almost as if there's a camera inside Jenny's belly."

"The new technology is amazing." He turned his attention to Jenny. "Are you all right?"

"It's wonderful." She spoke quietly, without taking her eyes off Lexie's image on the monitor. "Thank you."

"My pleasure," he chuckled. "You're healthy, and now

we know your baby is healthy, too. Keep up the good work."

On his way to the door he turned. "I'll let the technician take it from here. If you have any questions, don't hesitate to call me. I want to see you once a week until you deliver." He left the room in a flurry of white lab coat tails.

Jenny continued to watch the sonogram monitor. Matt continued to watch her.

He had to admit to an insatiable curiosity about the enigmatic mother of his child, and today he'd learned more from observing her than he'd ever learned from their conversations. He also saw in her a love, a longing, he didn't think he would ever see transferred to him.

It made him feel like an outsider, an interloper in what was obviously a moment of communion between mother and daughter.

The surge of joy he'd felt in seeing his child was overshadowed by something akin to despair. Jenny's claim she didn't need a man to make her life complete was confirmed by the life thriving inside her. He damned technology even as he reveled in its gifts.

A chill settled over his spirit that had nothing to do with the cold wind blowing outside. He wasn't sure he'd ever be warm again without these two beautiful women in his life.

Jenny couldn't see Matt behind her but felt him withdraw emotionally as the doctor left the room. It was almost as if he didn't want to talk to her anymore. She wondered if he was disappointed that the baby was not a boy.

Oh, she knew he'd gone along with her protestations that the baby was an Alexis and not a Matt, Jr., but she suspected he'd never really believed it.

At first he'd seemed fascinated by Lexie's image on the screen, but when they'd gotten down to the business of counting little fingers and toes and other tiny parts, or in Matt's case, tiny *missing* parts, he'd shifted back in his seat and become strangely quiet.

And nothing made her more uncomfortable than a strangely quiet Matt. Too much plotting went on inside that handsome head when he was quiet.

Worry aside, she knew it was best just to let him withdraw when he wanted to. Regardless of the way he kissed her, it was only a matter of time before he would walk away and she'd raise Lexie alone.

Yet it still took her by surprise when he stood, reached forward, and gave her fingers a squeeze. She drew their intertwined hands toward her belly, pressing playfully. The pressure caused Lexie to turn.

"Isn't she the most beautiful child you've ever seen? Hollywood is gonna come knocking before she's out of diapers, I swear it."

"I'd rather she had a normal childhood at home with her parents," Matt said softly.

"It doesn't always work out that way," Jenny replied, "but I'll do the best I can." She struggled to keep the wistful tone from her voice but failed. No one knew better than she how hard a not-normal childhood was on a kid.

Lexie, the ballerina/gymnast/kickboxing champ of Cincinnati, rolled in Jenny's belly and came to a stop facing the two people who loved her most. Jenny realized she, Matt and the baby might never be a family in truth, but here, today, they were close.

So close.

"She has your eyes," Jenny said, looking at Matt as tears filled her own.

"And your stubborn chin."

It was his harshest criticism yet. Jenny's excitement over the sonogram dimmed.

The technician helped Jenny sit up, then began the process of printing pictures of the baby.

Jenny slipped her arms into her jacket, then pulled it tight, like armor. "She's her mother's daughter, that's for sure."

Matt looked stricken, as if he'd realized what he'd said and how it hurt. She knew better than to expect an apology. He seemed frozen through.

He started to speak, but there wasn't much he could say that Jenny wanted to hear. His eyes left hers and went to the monitor where Lexie's image remained, suspended in time. "Then she's a very lucky little girl."

Night fell unusually early that evening, and the weather that was merely chilly during the morning had disintegrated to frigid by late afternoon. Matt could hardly believe he and Jenny had spent time talking on her front porch just twenty-four hours before.

Around nine o'clock the wind dropped and the clouds lowered menacingly. The icy rain started, thundering down from the heavens, quickly coating every surface. Southern Ohio ice storms always hit hard, fast and unexpectedly. This one was no exception. Ancient oaks and maples snapped, taking power lines with them. Neighborhoods all over the city lost electricity.

Never again could Matt claim his mother didn't raise any fools.

If a grown man racing a truck across a hilly town like Cincinnati in the aftermath of what seemed like the most dangerous ice storm in a century couldn't qualify for Fool of the Year, nobody could.

Steadman had left for a weekend vacation a few hours before the storm hit. He'd called to say he'd checked into a motel outside town, riding out the harsh weather.

His mother was safe and sound in her home across the river in Kentucky.

Now he had only Jenny to take care of. He glanced at the phone on the car seat next to him. He wanted desperately to pick it up and call her again. She hadn't answered his call an hour or so ago, and his fear for her well-being was like a knife in his gut. He was afraid to take his hands off the wheel, fearful of losing control of the vehicle. Anything that delayed getting to Jenny was not worth considering.

Without warning the truck went into a skid. It slid across the road, coming to a sudden, jarring stop next to a high curb. So much for the importance of two-handed driving. When he was sure he wasn't about to slide the rest of the way down the street, he thanked providence for slowing him down, picked up the phone and punched in Jenny's number. This time she answered.

"Where have you been?" He realized he was shouting. Lowering his voice he asked, "Are you all right?"

"Matt?" Her voice was vague and sleepy, his name accompanied by the chattering of teeth. She must have been sleeping, then awakened by his call.

"Something's wrong. The lights won't work and it's so cold."

"We've had an ice storm. A doozey. Stay inside and hang on, honey. I'm on my way."

He heard a noise, like the phone dropping to the floor. He began to shout her name again.

"Matt? I'm scared."

"Sweetheart, you're fine. The storm knocked out the power. Stay on the phone with me and I'll be there in a few minutes. Why don't you get a flashlight and use it to find a blanket and some extra socks. Wrap up good and tight so you don't get any colder."

"I'm going to have to put down the phone."

He heard a muted thump, then the sound of a drawer opening and closing. Another eternity passed before she picked up again.

"Okay. I'm all bundled up now. Where are you? Do you have your heavy coat on?

"I'm turning into your neighborhood now. Go to the front door and unlock it. Then I want you to get in bed."

He heard a gasp. "Matt," she said frostily. "I hardly think this is the time—"

"Sweetheart," he interrupted, using all the patience he could muster. "Get in bed so you'll be warmer. You have to conserve your body heat until I get there."

"Oh." He could have sworn her heard a note of disappointment in her voice.

The faint click of the lock reverberated over the phone. He followed her progress to the bedroom by the sound of shuffling feet.

"Matt?" The faraway quality of her voice terrified him. "If I fall asleep again will you wake me up?"

"Don't go to sleep, Jenny. It's very important that you stay awake. Can you hear me? *You have to stay awake.*"

"Okay. Don't yell, okay?"

"Talk to me, honey."

"What about?"

"I don't know. What about Maggie? Have you talked to her lately? How's Hope?"

"Hope? She said her first complete sentence the other day. Did I tell you that? She picked up her blankie, walked to the door and said, 'Hope go Ninny's.' Maggie was so happy. I can't wait until Lexie learns to talk."

Jenny sniffed and Matt knew she was about to cry.

"Do you think they're all right? The center is so old, I know it must be cold there."

"They're okay. On my way over here I could see the lights still on downtown. It's only in the outlying areas that the power is out."

"Good. Where are you now?"

"I'm pulling up in front of your house. You should see the cars out here. They look like big glass bugs."

Matt stopped the SUV and set the parking brake but left the motor and heater running. He flung himself out the door of the vehicle and made his way, slipping and sliding, up the sidewalk.

The house was frighteningly quiet when he stepped into the foyer. He trained his flashlight on the living room, then into the kitchen. He realized the center hallway would take him to the bedroom and Jenny.

A faint, wavering light came toward him through the darkness.

"Matt?" Jenny asked.

He pointed the beam of his flashlight at Jenny and froze. Even bundled up in blankets the heft of her belly was unmistakable.

"God help me," he mumbled. "I forgot she was pregnant."

He'd been terrified she would be harmed by the cold, and so intent on getting to her he'd risked his own life on the icy roads. Images of her had filled his heart and his mind, blocking out all thoughts of logic and safety.

He'd completely forgotten about the baby.

It was like being hit on the head with a brick—or maybe a very big icicle.

He loved her. Her. Not because of the baby, but because deep inside his soul he recognized her as his other half.

Little Jenny Ames had stolen his heart and tucked it neatly in her pocket.

And he knew he'd never get it back.

That knowledge, coupled with the strangely erotic way she waddled down the hall, ignited an undeniable need to hold her. He felt like a Neanderthal ready to wield his club, to conquer, claim and protect his woman, then drag her to his cave.

Matt placed his fingers over the lamp of his flashlight to cut the glare. The filtered light illuminated her pale face and blue-tinged lips.

And what could he, a red-blooded American male, do but warm her the only way he knew?

He put down his flashlight and held out his arms.

"Come here," he ordered softly. As soon as she was close enough, he unwound the wool scarf from his neck and wrapped it around hers. He used the scarf to pull her head toward his, and when she was within kissing range he pressed his lips to hers, gently covering her mouth with his. His tongue swept in and tangled lazily with hers. She returned the kiss, but only halfheartedly, as though she weren't really awake. Try as he might, he couldn't stir her blood the way he knew he needed to.

Her lips were cold, as if it were summer and she'd been sitting in the backyard drinking a frosty lemonade. But it wasn't summer, and he knew she wouldn't get any warmer without some concerted effort on his part.

"Come closer."

Jenny complied, but instead of stepping into the folds of his coat, as he had planned, she only bumped his belly with hers.

"I don't seem to fit," she said, a bit sadly.

"We fit fine, sweetheart," he replied softly. "Let me show you."

He kissed her again, this time with the intent of raising her internal temperature while his own crept dangerously high. Even tousled from sleep and disoriented by the cold, she was sexy and desirable.

His hands left the knotted ends of his scarf and traveled to her back, tugging her an additional millimeter toward him. He touched her hands. They were icy cold.

"Here. Put your hands under my sweater." He flinched as the cold from her fingers permeated his shirt. Maybe this warming thing wasn't going to be as easy as he'd thought.

Digging under her blankets, he found the hem of her sweater. He slipped his hands underneath and searched until fingers met skin. Cold skin. With a light, yet possessive touch he rubbed his hands across her back, hoping the friction would warm her.

It didn't.

"This is my fault."

"You don't have power over the weather, Matt."

"Not that. If you'd been with me, you wouldn't have gotten so cold."

"You can't be everywhere. It's not your responsibility."

"I don't want to be responsible for everyone. I want to be responsible for you."

His declaration didn't seem to touch her, but he buried

his disappointment and tightened his hold. She rested her head on his shoulder and shuddered violently.

"We've got to chase away those shivers, honey. The sooner we get you out of here and to my house, the better."

"Do you have electricity?"

"I've got something better. I've got a fireplace in my bedroom."

Only after she'd washed her face with the water Matt heated on his gas grill and brushed her teeth with the icy flow from the faucet did Jenny allow her thoughts to settle on the three things waiting for her outside the bathroom door: a blazing fire, a warm bed and Matt.

She would have gladly forgone the first two for a life-time in the latter's arms.

After all, this was the guy who'd saved her life, and that was no small accomplishment in Jenny's book.

The car heater had brought her out of her cold-induced stupor about halfway to Matt's house. She'd been amazed at the skill with which he'd driven the truck—although how anyone could call that queen's barge a truck, she didn't know. It made her feel she was important to him, essential in a way that almost made her preen with pride.

Pride she knew from experience would most likely go before a fall.

Jenny picked up the candle Matt had given her, then set it down again. It was large and ornate, yet strangely in harmony with everything else she had seen in the dimly lit home. She leaned forward to peer into the gilded mirror that hung over the vanity and saw a woman who simply didn't fit.

The candle reflected more than enough light to allow her to see her deficiencies.

The worn flannel pajamas she'd bought at the thrift store because the man-size jacket accommodated her belly were just the beginning.

She hated the thoughts that plagued her, but they persisted. Krystal McDonnough had stood before this mirror, not in flannel, Jenny knew in her heart, but in silk and lace, preparing to go to Matt...pretty, perfect, *skinny.*

She glared at her reflection, a wry smile tipping up the corner of her mouth. "A little bit late to be worrying about your figure, isn't it?"

"Are you all right in there?"

"I'm just as I always have been," she muttered, reaching for the doorknob.

When she stepped out of the bathroom, her feet sank into plush carpet. Walking toward the bed, she buttoned her cuffs, keeping her hands busy so Matt wouldn't see them shaking. He'd turned back the bedspread, but she could tell without touching that it was watered silk. It was like touring a museum exhibit, except that all of it was real. Especially Matt.

And Matt's very masculine, muscled chest.

Her eyes widened when she saw that broad expanse of tanned flesh. Now in addition to their shaking, her hands itched to touch him. "Aren't you cold?"

"Yeah, but I hate pajamas. How about coming on over here and sharing a little body heat with me?"

"I can't."

"Why not?"

Why not, indeed. She was a grown woman in love with a grown man, and she was ready to share more than body heat. There was the little matter of her heart that needed to be taken care of tonight. "You're on my side of the bed."

"How do you figure that?"

"I always sleep on my left side, on the right side of the bed. It's better for the baby."

Matt stood, and she felt a moment of relief—and an even longer moment of regret—to see that he wore a pair of baggy sweatpants.

"Jump in, then," he said. "The sooner we get you comfortable, the better."

Jenny wanted to ask what would happen once she was comfortable but hesitated. Her inexperience was showing again, as it had when Matt kissed her for the first time and she'd booted him out of her office. Well, she wouldn't send him away tonight. She'd hold him close, and it wouldn't be just for his body heat.

Matt took her candle and set it on the bedside table. He lifted a pile of blankets and eased her into the huge Edwardian sleigh bed. Jenny set about arranging pillows and covers as Matt circled the bed. When he climbed in and snuggled close, her heart did a little flip.

There was no way she was going to get any sleep tonight, she thought as Matt guided her head to his shoulder. Not in his house, his bed. She said a small prayer for the beginning of a new ice age, closed her eyes and, quite surprisingly, drifted off to sleep, secure in the warm embrace of the man who'd captured her heart simply because he cared.

Chapter Twelve

Matt watched Jenny fall asleep. Her skin was much warmer now, and her breathing was steady and deep. Occasionally she would shift and mumble, but finally she burrowed into him and drifted deeper into sleep.

Her exertions worked loose all but one of the buttons on her threadbare pajama jacket. He'd made do with brief glimpses of her so far; the saucy knees that got uncovered every time she'd climbed into his car, the smooth curve of the shoulder he'd spied at his office. After he'd bared her belly he'd stayed awake all night contemplating the pink elastic edging of her panties. And now he had her in his bed. While not all the secrets of her body were laid bare, he had plenty of time—and the inclination—to uncover the rest.

He wanted to make love to her, wanted it more than anything he could imagine. He'd even asked Dan about it, but the doctor had merely shaken his head and frowned, so Matt let the subject drop. That didn't mean he didn't think about it, though.

He thought about it a lot.

Jenny muttered, then rolled onto her back. She flung her arms out, barely missing Matt's nose with her hand. The last small white button holding her pajama top together taunted him. Like the climber who tackled a mountain because it was there, he burned to see what lay beneath the plaid fabric. When he slipped his hand beneath the flannel his fingers encountered taut, silky skin. Jenny woke with a start and grabbed his hand.

"Is it morning?" she asked. The sleepy, husky quality of her voice reverberated through him, making him want her even more.

"No. I didn't mean to wake you. I just wanted to do this."

He leaned forward to kiss her, taking her by surprise. When her lips opened on a soft gasp he swooped in to capture them, making them his own. He reveled in Jenny's tiny gasps and sighs. His body responded to the love sounds, growing hard and taut. He wanted her with an intensity that astonished him. Never before had he felt this urgency, even with his fiancée. Never again would he question what love was.

He kissed her again, more deeply this time, then softly, until he drew back, struggling for his own breath.

"Sweetheart? I'm going to ask you a question and I want you to tell me the truth."

Jenny lowered her eyes, knowing instinctively what he was going to ask. She'd put everything she had into those kisses, but he was a man of the world, and he knew. Her experience, or lack thereof, was about to become the topic of a conversation she'd hoped to avoid.

Although how she thought she was going to manage it while she lay beside him, his hand resting seductively atop her belly, she couldn't quite figure.

"The naked truth?" She hoped her question held the perfect combination of playfulness and sensuality.

Matt laughed, sending a thrill of erotic warmth running throughout her body.

"I wish," he said.

"What do you want to know?"

"Have you ever, uh, shared body heat with a man before?"

For a moment it was quiet in the room, the crackling of the fire the only sound.

"Are you asking me if I'm a virgin?"

"I take it back," he said quickly. The soft candlelight from the bedside table illuminated his blush. "You don't have to tell me."

"I want to. I'm not ashamed of the truth." She'd known he would be gentle, in both his words and his actions, but she'd never dreamed simply lying next to him would be so extraordinary. She felt utterly feminine and cherished. She rested her hand on his. "I didn't date until I went to college. I would see the other girls around campus with their boyfriends, holding hands and walking to and from class. I wanted to be like them. Maybe I was a little jealous."

"I think there was more to it," he said, as if he knew her innermost secrets.

"I didn't want to be afraid anymore. For a long time I thought maybe what happened to me in Australia had warped me. Everybody talked about sex like it was so great, but all I knew was the shame. I wanted to know what it was all about. All the fuss, I mean."

"Fuss?" He rolled her onto her side to face him. She tried lowering her gaze to the barely visible pulse beat at the hollow of his throat, but he used his finger to lever her chin back up.

"Fuss?"

"You know." Her voice dropped to a whisper. "Orgasms."

"Oh," he said quietly. "And what did you learn about orgasms."

"Nothing."

"What are you saying?" His voice rose, and the sound reverberated off the walls of the darkened room. "You had sex with a guy and he didn't even give you an orgasm?"

She shook her head sadly. "We were in his dorm room and he was afraid we'd get caught. It happened so fast…it wasn't very good. He didn't even kiss me."

Matt raised up on one arm and glared down into her eyes. "What's this guy's name? We need to get him off the streets before he disappoints another woman."

"Too late. He got married about six months after graduation."

"Poor girl."

"You don't know the half of it. Nancy knows his secretary. She says they're having an affair."

"That bastard!"

Jenny laughed. "You believed that?" She poked him in the chest. "I'm a better storyteller than I thought. I don't know where he is, Matt. And I don't care."

"He cheated you, Jenny."

"No, he didn't. We were using each other. Nobody got shortchanged because neither of us deserved for anything special to come of it."

"How did you get to be so wise?"

"I've had a lot of time to think about it. I've learned there are certain things in life people aren't meant to have, no matter how much they want them."

"I don't want you to settle, Jenny. You deserve the best."

"I have everything I need, Matt, now that I've met you."

He held her in his arms, cradling her like a baby. A storm may have raged outside, but with Matt she felt safe. A feeling of peace surrounded her, and she knew perfect happiness for the first time.

She awoke in his arms, warm as toast. The blaze in the fireplace had burned down to embers, but the blankets around them still held their heat. It might have had something to do with Matt's body curled neatly around hers, or it might have been the fullness of her heart.

Matt brought out all the emotions she'd so carefully bundled up and stored away when she decided to live her life as a single woman.

But what now?

Letting herself think there was anything more to their relationship than a little shared body heat would be disastrous, at least until she knew how he felt.

Men were slow to commit. Everybody said so. Maybe Matt was waiting for some word from her.

Jenny allowed her eyes to drift closed and listened to the silence deep inside her heart. No help from her grandmothers in that quarter. No surprise there. She'd never believed they knew anything about love.

Everything she knew about love she'd learned from Alexis and Matt. And it was time to tell him so.

Her skin prickled with the feeling of being watched. She opened her eyes and looked into Matt's.

"Good morning, beautiful." He leaned in to kiss her,

letting his lips dance lightly over hers. "I thought you looked good by firelight, but you're absolutely magnificent in the light of day."

His hands, warm from sleep, traced softly up and down her back.

"Mmmm. You feel good. How did you sleep?"

"Matt—"

In lieu of an answer, he dipped his mouth to the curve of her neck and shoulder, scattering kisses across her skin, making a rambling path to the V of her pajamas, to her nearly exposed breasts. Through the soft fabric he took a pebbled nipple between his lips and teased. His suckling mouth shot a sweet sensation of wanting through her, creating a need for him that she felt in every cell of her being.

"Matt—"

The silence of the room and the icy world outside was shattered by the revving of a chain saw and the shouts of masculine voices.

"Sounds like the cleanup has started." He dropped a quick kiss on her mouth and rolled onto his back. "Will you be all right while I go take a look?"

Jenny waited until he'd dressed and left the room before she gave her tears full reign. Nothing was going as she had planned.

Well, maybe *planned* wasn't exactly the right word for it. She hadn't really planned anything past telling Matt she loved him and then, she hoped, hearing that he loved her, too.

And what had she expected, really?

Any gesture, even a small one, would have been better than his running out to play with a bunch of lumberjack wannabes.

Disappointed beyond words, she left the bed and took an icy sponge bath. After she'd dressed she sat by the window, waiting for Matt to return. When he did, he carried steaming hot coffee and warm Danish.

"One of the guys down the street has a motor home. His wife got up early this morning and cooked for the cleanup crew. I told them I had company, so she sent breakfast home with me."

A startled gasp escaped her. "You told them about me?"

"Yeah. Everybody knows about the baby. I wanted them to know. They're my neighbors."

"B-but—" she sputtered.

"Your neighbors know about me, don't they?"

"How could they miss you? It's not every day someone pulls up in front of my house in a limousine. No, I take that back. It *is* every day, even weekends."

"Look, Jenny," he said in a placating tone, "we both value our privacy, but it's a little late to be trying to keep this a secret."

"I wish things were more settled." Her breath quickened and she felt her cheeks grow warm. She was angry with herself for being embarrassed. She wanted to be brave. She wanted to be different, able to set aside her fears and trust, but like the old dog who couldn't learn a new trick, she hung her head.

"There may be a solution to that problem," he said slowly.

Jenny's head jerked up and she looked at Matt, not even trying to hide the love in her eyes. Against her will she dared to hope.

"I think it would be a good idea if you stayed with me until the baby's born."

It shouldn't have surprised her, that familiar feeling

of her heart breaking. It was the same as before. No, a little worse this time…much worse.

It was the same painful sinking feeling she'd felt as she stood on the tarmac of a dusty Australian airport, waiting for the parents who never came to say goodbye.

The same dreadful anticipation of waiting for the phone that didn't ring after she'd given herself to her college sweetheart. To yet another man who didn't love her.

Why didn't anyone want her?

History repeated itself. That was the story, chapter and verse of Jenny Ames's life.

She felt another rush of embarrassment flush her cheeks. Swallowing her tears, she stood quickly and turned away from Matt, hoping to hide her reaction to his cold-blooded invitation. He couldn't have known she was praying for a declaration of love, maybe even a marriage proposal.

How could she have been such a fool? Wouldn't you think she'd have learned by now?

Jenny laughed, although not even she was convinced by the levity. She swung around, and the weight of her belly nearly sent her spinning. Her hand rested on the knob of the closet door. "Thanks for the invitation, Matt, but I couldn't possibly live in a place this opulent. My goodness, I bet you have more closets than the White House. I could probably fit my entire house inside this bedroom."

She flung open a door. "A whole room just for neckties? And another for shoes? Hey, I didn't know you wore cowboy boots."

She chattered nervously as she made her way around the room. Matt watched her with a look that said he thought she'd lost her mind. A small door by the back window wall caught her eye. She moved toward it, barely noticing him leap to his feet and race across the room.

"What's this one for?" she asked as she turned the knob. "Hats?"

"Jenny, no!"

She ignored his cry and turned to look into the small room.

Inside, the only hat visible was a miniature one decorated with pink roses and ivory ribbons. It hung on the wall next to an elegant cradle Jenny knew cost a small fortune. It made the sturdy white crib she'd chosen for Alexis at the secondhand furniture store look like the cheap junk it was.

In the corner sat an antique rocker upholstered in rose-colored moiré silk, just waiting for father and child. Disposable diapers, baby powder and wipes waited on the changing table.

The louvered doors of the closet stood open, revealing a row of tiny dresses and expensive coordinated outfits, shoes and bonnets included. There was even a pair of sneakers like Hope's.

Jenny walked slowly around the room, touching each item.

She turned to him, tears streaming down her cheeks. "How could you? You planned this all along, didn't you? All those times you invited me here it was to trick me into staying. What were you going to do? Change the locks while I was at work? Have Mr. Steadman drop me off in the country like a stray kitten?"

Her voice rose hysterically. "Everyone tried to warn me, even Krystal. They all said you'd do anything to get what you want, and I can see they were right."

She turned in a circle, looking for an escape route.

Spotting a door she was sure led to the hall, she raced for it. "You'll never take my baby, Matt Hanson. I'll do whatever I have to to stop you, even run to the other side of the globe."

"Jenny, stop!" Matt followed her out to the hall. "You've completely misunderstood. Let me explain."

She wasn't about to wait around for explanations. Based on what she'd seen, Matt was a man waiting to bring his new baby home.

Everything was ready and waiting for the child, but nowhere in the house did she see a place for its mother.

"Let him get his own baby, damn it. He sure as hell isn't going to get mine," she muttered angrily.

She ran toward the staircase, not caring that she'd forgotten to put on her shoes or grab her coat. She didn't care that she didn't have a way home, either. She only knew she had to get as far away from Matt as she could before he could take her baby.

As she lunged toward the steps her belly swung out in front of her, throwing her off balance. She grabbed the wooden railing, but the socks she wore couldn't gain purchase on the heavily waxed floor. Her feet began to slide. Her heels glanced off the front edge of the top riser and she began to trip, one foot over the other, toward the bottom of the steps. Only her grip on the banister saved her from a deadly free fall.

As Jenny fell, Matt saw his life flash before his eyes, but with a twist. All the scenes were of her.

Jenny on the day they met, her hand laid protectively over her belly.

Jenny eating raspberry-chocolate ice cream.

Jenny in his bed.

Jenny in his heart.

As he raced down the stairs behind her, he prayed for a miracle, one in which neither of the special women in his life was injured.

He must have done something right, because just at that moment Jenny got a grip on the banister and landed smack on her butt only inches from the gleaming marble of the foyer floor.

Chapter Thirteen

"Jenny," Matt shouted as he skidded to a painful halt on his knees next to her. "Talk to me. Are you all right?"

Her face was chalky white and her eyes were tightly squeezed together. She sat upright, clinging to the banister.

"The baby, Matt," she sobbed. "The baby."

He barely remembered grabbing the phone and dialing Dan's number, or begging him to come to their aid. He threw open the front door and raced back to Jenny.

By the time Dan arrived, Matt had managed to pry Jenny's hands off the banister and place them around his neck. He'd wanted to disobey the doctor's order not to move her, but instead merely held her, rubbing her back as soothingly as he could. While they waited, Jenny cried.

Dan climbed a single step and squatted in front of Jenny.

"Jenny," he said with an easy calm, "when I said I wanted to see you every week, this is not what I meant."

Jenny gave him a watery smile and wiped her tears with the sleeve of her sweater.

"Can you tell me what happened?"

She moved her arms from Matt's neck and inched away from him as if she'd just remembered where she was and how she got there. "My feet slipped and I fell."

He took her hand. "You understand I have to ask this." He glanced at Matt, then back to Jenny. "Were you pushed?"

Jenny's voice dropped to a whisper. "No. We argued, but it was my fault that I fell. Matt was in the...the nursery."

"At any time during your fall, did your belly strike the stairs, or the banister?"

"No. I didn't hit anything until I landed on my butt."

"No pain or cramping in your belly?"

"None."

"What do you say we take a little inventory before we move you? Can you do that for me?"

At Jenny's nod, Dan began checking for injuries. "Does your head hurt?"

"No."

"Your neck? How about arms and shoulders? Any numbness in your hands? Wiggle your fingers. That's good."

Matt watched Jenny flex her wrists, and he flexed his own, willing her joints to work as well as his. She bent her elbows and shrugged her shoulders. Matt followed suit. Dan pulled off her socks, rotated her ankles and tested each of her toes for breaks. Despite the seriousness of the situation, and completely ignoring the fact that

Dan was his best friend and Jenny's doctor, Matt fumed at the fact the man was daring to touch his woman.

Matt grew frantic. In a last desperate attempt to claim Jenny as his, he blurted out, "She slept in my bed last night."

"Matt!" Finally Jenny was looking at him, not Dan. And that color staining her cheeks was a good sign, wasn't it?

"I don't think that was a factor in Jenny's fall," Dan said dryly. "Why don't you settle down a little? Go fire up the grill and boil some water."

"Oh, God!" he shrieked. "The baby's coming now?"

"No, the baby's not coming. You need something to do and I'd like a cup of coffee." Dan gave him a "get lost" look. "Give the lady some privacy, Hanson."

By the time Matt got back with Dan's coffee, Jenny was resting in a recliner in the living room.

"I've told Jenny she'll probably have a backache for a few days, but my cursory examination shows no injuries to her or the baby. The womb is amazingly like a giant shock absorber. It's rare for a baby to be injured in a simple slip and fall like this, even if Mom feels like she's been tossed around in a cement mixer."

He turned back to Jenny. "I was getting ready to touch base with the hospital when Matt called. I'll go take care of that, then come back and check on you again in about an hour. If you have any pain or bleeding, call 911."

"But the ambulance can't get here—"

"The temperature's rising, and the ice is melting. The streets should be clear by noon."

Almost as punctuation to the doctor's comment on the passing of the storm, Jenny heard the *whump* of the furnace coming on. The clock on the DVD player began to flash.

The look on Matt's face told her the power was probably on at her house, too.

"I want to go home." She struggled to sit up.

"No!" Both men answered at the same time. Matt's tone was panicked, Dr. Wilson's stern. They stood, shoulder to shoulder, a united front, blocking her access to the door.

Jenny knew it was time to back down, if not for her own sake, then for the baby's. But she would go home, and she would take up her life where she was before she met Matt Hanson, and she would be happy again.

Or at least as happy as she could be with a broken heart.

Morning turned into afternoon, and in early evening Dan Wilson said Jenny could leave. Matt unwillingly gathered her things and took her home. The distance between them had become so great Matt felt she might was well be living on another continent instead of a few miles across town.

All the things he should have done and all the things he should have said—"Do you mind if I decorate a room for the baby?" being primary—swirled through his head.

He really thought Jenny had gotten over her worries about his intentions to take the baby away from her. That's why he'd called in an interior designer to do the nursery. That's why the bed in the guest room was strewn with fabric and drapery and carpet samples, all in shades of blue, so that Jenny could pick what she wanted for the room she would stay in when Alexis visited. *If* Jenny would let her visit.

It was all he could think to do in light of her absolute refusal to discuss a permanent relationship between them.

And now, discussion of any sort was completely out of the question. Jenny had gone glacial. He stole a look at her from the corner of his eye. Where was his little wildcat now?

It would take years to sort out all his feelings, yet the baby would arrive within a few weeks. Everything would be so much easier if Jenny would just tell him what he'd done wrong!

But that would be too easy. He'd obviously screwed up big-time, and Jenny had nearly paid the price with her life.

Ah, Jenny. He glanced again at his silent companion. The reason behind her refusal to speak to him was obvious. She used her anger to shield herself from hurt. If she refused to listen, she was unlikely to hear something that didn't jibe with all her preconceived notions.

That was fine. It was her right to be as angry as she liked.

He'd give her a day, okay, two, to cool off, then he'd be back there swinging. No way was he letting her go.

Not now, not ever.

When he pulled up in front of her house, Jenny immediately reached for the door handle. He leaned across to stop her.

"Don't even think about it. You sit right there until I get around to the door."

She leaned back and made a show of unbuckling her seat belt and digging in her purse for her key, all without looking at him. But she stayed put.

On the porch he held his hand out for the key, but she clutched it, unlocking the door with white-knuckled

fingers. She stepped inside, apparently planning to slam
the door in his face. Matt pressed his hand against the
frame, stopping her.

"Jenny," he said softly. "I'm sorry for the things that
happened today. Please don't be angry at me."

She shook her head sadly.

He knew it was crunch time. This could be the last
opportunity he might have to speak to her as a friend.
The next words that came out of his mouth had the
power to make or break both their hearts.

"Jen." This time he whispered. "If men were the ones
who got pregnant…if I was the one who was carrying
your child, would you let me go?"

She stepped back and closed the door, but he heard
her answer and knew it for the lie it was.

"Yes."

Jenny spent the next two days crying. The tearful
woman she saw in the mirror had no resemblance whatsoever to the stoic child she'd been. When she was
younger, when her grandmother died and her parents
abandoned her, tears were not an acceptable form of
grief in her great-grandmother's household. She'd
learned to hide her feelings. In her work, especially
with the children, it was easy to become overwhelmed
by emotion.

But this was not work. It was her life and she was
miserable and she was going to wallow in it if she darn
well pleased.

By the third day she was sick of crying. Nothing had
been accomplished by it, unless you counted that her
ankles were no longer swollen because she was dehy-
drated.

And she was lonely, too. Lonely for Matt.

The knock at her door came as no surprise. She'd been waiting for Matt, anticipating, dreading, praying for his visit. He wasn't the type to give up, regardless of how mad she got. That was probably one of the things she loved best about him.

But the visitor wasn't Matt. He'd sent in reinforcements.

"You must be Mrs. Hanson," Jenny said. "The brown eyes gave you away."

The older woman smiled Matt's smile and reached out to shake Jenny's hand. She reminded Jenny of a TV mother...one who laughed indulgently at her children's antics and cooked dinner wearing pearls and an apron.

"Please call me Elaine."

Jenny stepped back. "Would you like to come in?"

Matt's mother seemed shocked by Jenny's warm greeting; eager to be invited in, but wary, too.

"I won't stay long, I promise. You must be busy, getting ready for the baby and all. I brought this for Alexis." She handed Jenny a package wrapped in pink ribbons. "And this is for you."

Matt's mother drew an old photograph album from under her arm. It reminded Jenny of the one that held her own childhood pictures.

She put down the baby's present and balanced the album on her belly. She opened it and slowly began to page through Matt's history, photo by photo.

Elaine pointed to a shot of Matt at a Boy Scout function. A tall man stood by his side. "This one was taken two weeks before Matt's father died." She turned the page. "This is his school picture, taken about a month after the funeral. When I look at these pictures I barely recognize my little boy.

"Matt was very affected by his father's death. He felt as if he'd been abandoned. My husband, Jack, was a classic workaholic. He wanted the very best for his family and thought success was the way to get it. Matt is very much his father's son. When I heard about you and your baby I hoped he would find the strength to change. But I fear he's only become more set in his ways."

"Elaine, I think you know your little boy very well."

"How can I convince you to give him another chance?"

"I don't know if I can. He and I are too far apart on a lot of issues that are really important to me." Like honesty and openness. Like love and marriage.

"He's hurt you."

"Yes."

"You love him, don't you?"

It seemed pointless to deny it. She closed the album. "I love him very much."

"Mr. Hanson? Ms. Ames is here and would like to see you."

"Jenny? Here?" Matt jumped to his feet. He could barely contain his joy. The past week, seven long days without Jenny in them, had barely been worth living.

"Where is she?"

"In the conference room with Mr. McBride."

"What's Greg doing with her?"

"He brought her in, sir."

He struggled into his jacket and straightened his tie. Although he'd scarcely been alive without Jenny around, it wouldn't do to look it. He had to appear to be the kind of man she would want in her life. Hopefully, that was what she was here to tell him.

But why the lawyer?

His lawyer.

Jenny wore blue, the dress she'd had on when he'd kissed her for the first time, and looked so beautiful it almost made his heart stand still. The ribbon ties on each side were let all the way out to accommodate her expanding middle. All Matt's protective instincts came to the fore at the sight of the woman he loved more than life, despite the fact she'd turned him inside out, then tied him up in knots.

Jenny glanced up and caught him staring. She looked tired. Matt felt his heart clench in his chest. This was all his fault, the weary look, the sad eyes. All of it.

"I asked Mr. McBride…Greg, to come here with me today. I hope you won't be angry with him for helping me."

"Of course not," Matt said congenially, a fake smile on his face, but the look he gave Greg let him know there would be consequences if things didn't go well.

"We've prepared a document I'd like you to look at."

"A restraining order?" he asked, his heart in his throat.

"No, of course not." Jenny sounded genuinely surprised. "I don't want to hurt you, Matt. That's why I asked Greg to be my attorney. I knew he would look out for your interests as well as mine."

"I don't understand."

Jenny dropped back in her chair and looked at Greg for assistance.

"Jenny asked me to prepare an agreement giving you joint custody of Alexis Elaine Ames with the understanding that you won't sue for full custody at a later date. She asks only that you not take the baby out of the city without notifying her first. In return, she agrees to the same stipulation."

Matt turned to Jenny. "Why?"

"Isn't it what you want?"

"It's more than I'd ever hoped for. But what about you?"

"I want what's best for all of us. You're a good and honest man. I know if you sign this agreement, you'll abide by it. Then I won't have to worry about Lexie, ever."

Matt had never been so frustrated. "You know, if you would just m—"

She cut him off cold. "This is the best I can do, Matt. Take it or leave it."

He looked at the agreement Greg had placed on the table. This was not what he expected, that the times they'd spent together would be reduced to a few pieces of paper and an agreement he didn't really want.

Jenny rose from her chair and walked to the window. The morning light streaming through the glass lit her and made her look more like a madonna than ever before.

He walked to her and offered up his handkerchief. She laughed ruefully at the sight of it, remembering, no doubt, the number of times he'd rescued her without one.

"You probably think I cry all the time. But I don't. I never cry."

He tipped her chin toward him. "I can't bear to see you like this. Tell me what to do to make you smile again."

"Will you move to Siberia and never come back?"

"No, sweetheart, I can't do that. You and I are bound together forever by that little bump in your tummy. Even if I went to the dark side of the moon, I'd still be in your life. I want to know my daughter. Is that such a terrible thing?"

"No, it's not a terrible thing. You'll be a wonderful father. You had a great teacher."

"How do you know that?"

"Your mother came to see me. She told me about your dad, about the suddenness of the heart attack. I know how it must have felt to lose him like that."

"You felt that way, too, didn't you? When you were sixteen?"

Jenny turned back to the window. A look of wistfulness clouded her face. "She's an amazing woman, your mother. You're lucky to have her."

He felt the beginnings of a smile tip the corners of his mouth. It had been so long, he'd thought he'd forgotten how. "Alexis Elaine, huh?"

Jenny nodded. "Every little girl should have a grandmother who loves her, you know?"

Another tear made its way down Jenny's cheek. Matt held out his arms and Jenny stepped into his embrace. She rested her head against his shoulder.

"I'm so sorry, Jenny. I never meant for any of this to happen, but I swear, if I had to do it over again, I wouldn't change a thing."

"I know. Me, neither." She backed away and picked up her purse from the conference table. "I would appreciate it if you wouldn't contact me. I have a lot of thinking to do and it would be best if I did it alone."

"What about the labor? Will you let me coach you?"

Jenny shrugged. "I don't know." The corner of her mouth lifted in a mournful smile. "Another thing to add to my list."

"If you need anything, will you call me?"

She nodded.

"Will you let Steadman take you home?"

"Yes, please, but this will have to be the last time. I need to start taking care of myself again."

As she turned to leave the room he reached for her and took her hand. He drew her back toward him, and by some miracle, in spite of her bulk, they fit together perfectly. He bent his head and covered her mouth with his. He hoped his kiss would tell her everything she needed to know without him having to say a word.

Nothing that went before, the anger or the possession or even the lust, was represented in this kiss. Parting her lips, Jenny raised herself to meet him, and the moment they shared was one of reconciliation. Reluctantly he let her go. The door closed behind her, and Matt heard Greg clear his throat.

"I don't get it."

"Get what?" Matt asked.

"She's miserable, you're miserable. The two of you are so sappy in love seeing you together just now ran my blood sugar up at least a thousand points. Not to mention at the same time it damn near made me cry. And I'm a cold-blooded lawyer-type. Imagine what all that schmaltz would do to a regular guy with a real heart?"

"Trust me, pal. It's better not to have a heart in situations like this." He pounded a fist against his chest. "This breaking feeling is a real bitch."

Matt picked up the documents and shuffled them, not really reading the words but trying to get a sense of what had happened and why Jenny was willing to share Alexis's custody. He slid them across the polished surface of the table toward Greg. Then he looked for something to throw.

"I used to think I was a pretty smart guy, but this

whole thing has got me buffaloed." He pointed toward the door. "Why is this woman not my wife? If she can trust me with Alexis, why can't she trust me with her heart?"

"Aren't you going after her?"

"Not this time. I've chased her up hill and down valley since the day we met and look where it's gotten me. This time I'm going to wait until I figure out what the hell it is I'm doing wrong."

"Do you have any idea what happened?"

"Not a clue."

"Well, that's helpful. Let's go back to the beginning. Exactly what did you say when you asked her to marry you?"

Matt's eyes cut toward Greg, then closed slowly. He rested his head in the palm of his hand. Slowly Matt looked at his friend, his eyes burning with anger and embarrassment. "I'm an idiot. I've been so busy reaching for the brass ring, I forgot to ask the lady what she wanted."

He straightened and rested his hands on his hips. "I said, to the love of my life and the mother of my child—oh, wait a minute, let me get this right. I need just the perfect tone of butt-headed arrogance in my voice. I said, "'I think we should get married.'"

"Nice," Greg commented dryly. "I can see how a woman like Jenny would fall right into your arms after a declaration like that."

"That can't be it," Matt said, shaking his head. "She can *not* have walked out of my life because I didn't make some grand show out of asking her to marry me."

"Do this for me, Matt. Give me one word that describes the kind of woman Jenny Ames is. One word.

It's a technique my old law professor used to boil a problem down to its essence. If you can do that, I think you'll understand what you have to do."

Matt thought of all the things Jenny was, of what she'd brought to his life.

Beautiful? Too easy.

Generous? Everyone who knew her knew that.

Compassionate? Intelligent? Constant?

Any man lucky enough to win her would be content for the rest of his life.

"Forever," he said in a tone filled with awe and recognition, and just a hint of inspiration. "Jenny's a forever kind of woman."

Greg grinned. "You got that right, buddy."

The Monday after Elaine's visit Jenny stood with her neighbors and watched as the Metro bus chugged up the hill to their stop. Each of them had welcomed her back to the fold warmly, and the sense of familiarity and continuity that surrounded the little group made some of her apprehensions fade away.

Now her only worry was that she would be too broad to make it through the vehicle's door.

The huge coach slid to a stop before her. With a hiss, the doors opened wide. The driver greeted her with a smile, then his eyes slid to a passenger standing at the top of the stairs.

It was unusual, but not unheard of, for someone to get off the bus that early in the day. Jenny stepped back to make room for his departure.

But the passenger did not disembark. He stood on the bottom step, unmoving.

Jenny felt the hairs on the back of her neck lift. She

raised her eyes from the loafer-clad feet to skim the sharp creases of dark suit pants, the deep-red tones of the silk necktie against the stark white of a dress shirt, and on to Matt's beloved face.

She'd missed him desperately, been alternately furious and devastated. How she could have fallen so deeply in love with a man she'd known barely two months was a mystery she might never solve. But that didn't matter now. He was here. She couldn't hold back her smile.

Matt stepped down from the bus and held out a bouquet of pink roses and baby's breath.

"I know you said no flowers, but I hope you'll forgive me. I hope you'll forgive me for a lot of things."

Jenny buried her nose in the bouquet and breathed in the heavenly scent. Tears gathered at the corners of her eyes.

A gasp rose from the others gathered there at the sight of Jenny's tears. Along with the wide eyes and opened mouths of Jenny's fellow passengers there was a sense of alarm.

"What's the meaning of this?" one of the older women asked. "Who are you?"

He took Jenny's hand and addressed the small crowd. "My name is Matt Hanson, and if you good people will bear with me for a few minutes, I'll soon be Ms. Ames's fiancé."

"My what?"

He looked back at her and grinned. "Jenny, there's something I've been meaning to ask you since the day we met."

As her heart leaped, all her worries and apprehensions fled. She knew, without him having to say the words, why he was there. This was the Matt she loved, had loved forever, it seemed.

"There's something I've been meaning to tell you, but I've been afraid," she said quietly.

She stepped into his arms and whispered in his ear.

"What did she say?" Mrs. Harvey asked.

"Shh," Mrs. Simpson chided.

"Well, I want to hear. This is the most interesting thing that's happened in this neighborhood since the tornado back in ninety-nine."

Jenny giggled and leaned back into the circle of Matt's arms. She turned toward her neighbors. "I said I love him."

She searched his eyes for acceptance. He rewarded her honesty with a kiss. "That's a good thing, isn't it?" she asked.

"It will make what I have to say a lot easier, knowing that."

"Then get on with it, young man," Mr. Baxter interjected. "What do you have to say for yourself?"

"I love her, too."

"And?" Mrs. Simpson stood with all Jenny's other neighbors. The bus riders were lowering the windows, hanging out to see the circus Matt had brought to their street. He could see that proposing to Jenny had become a community event, and, really, who was he to spoil their fun?

He took Jenny's hand and lowered himself to his right knee. When he glanced up he saw that she had caught her lower lip with her small white teeth and her chin was beginning to quiver.

"Jenny, my love—"

"Wait!" she cried.

Matt dropped his head. "Oh, God, baby. Don't do this to me."

"Look." She pointed to the white limo that pulled to a stop behind the bus. The doors swung open and Mr. Steadman climbed out along with Greg, Nancy, Matt's secretary and his mother. Maggie and Hope Turner followed. A silver Lexus stopped behind the limo. Dan Wilson emerged.

"Am I too late? I had to reschedule a couple of appointments so I could get here on time."

Jenny's eyes widened. "You invited people to hear you propose? In public?"

"I wanted witnesses, sweetheart. Friends who know I cherish you and want to marry you. People who can remind you, if you ever lose faith in me, that I'll always love you, no matter what."

"Was that it?" Mrs. Harvey asked with a sputter of disappointment. "Not much of a proposal, if you ask me."

Mrs. Simpson concurred. "I prefer a more traditional approach, myself."

Matt cleared his throat. "Ladies and gentlemen, if I could have your attention. *Please.*"

He turned back to Jenny, who was struggling not to laugh. He swallowed his own mirth. "Honey, please don't. I want to get this right."

He took her hand again and pressed a chaste kiss upon it. Then he looked into her beautiful eyes and wondered why he'd waited so long for this moment.

"Jenny, will you marry me? I love you more than I ever thought it was possible for a man to love a woman. I want to be your husband and a father to our child. I want to share a cloud with you in heaven and never, ever regret the circumstances of our meeting."

Jenny, uncharacteristically, was unable to speak. Matt took a heart-shaped sapphire ring out of its box and slid it on her finger. She began to sob. Matt pulled her into his arms and made a silent promise never to let her go.

"Will you marry me? Say you'll marry me, Jenny."

Jenny tucked her face into the hollow of his neck.

"Just nod if it's yes, sweetheart. If it's no, shoot me now. I don't want to live without you."

Jenny nodded.

Matt let out a whoop that might have been heard all the way to the state line.

The crowed roared.

He covered her mouth with his and sealed the deal with a lingering kiss.

The bus driver blew his horn as the neighbors applauded.

Jenny laughed, hiccuped and laughed again. She put her hands on her huge belly and said, "Lexie says yes, too."

"Speaking of Lexie, do you think we could get married *before* she's born? I'd like all three of our last names to be the same on the birth certificate."

"I know a judge," Greg offered helpfully.

"And I've got a mother who's dying to organize an overnight wedding," Matt said, laughing.

"I guess the only other question is who'll give the bride away," Elaine said as John Steadman, Dan Wilson and Greg McBride all lined up behind Jenny.

The bride-to-be laughed. "Too late, gentlemen." She took Matt's hand and clutched it to her breast. "I'm already gone."

Epilogue

Jenny and Matt were married at Matt's house a week later. Jenny wore pale blue and carried pink roses with baby's breath. Matt took her breath away—and the breath of every other woman in the room—in his tuxedo.

They stood on the steps, the second one from the bottom, and faced their guests so that, according to Jenny's wishes, everyone could see how happy they were.

Greg brought the judge, an older, slightly round man who reminded Jenny of Mickey Rooney.

"We are gathered here today," he said solemnly, "to join this man and woman together in holy matrimony. They are committed to one another in love and in anticipation of the child who personifies the best of both of them. A new family is created today, and the world is better for it."

"We're a real family now," Jenny whispered.

"Yes," Matt replied. "And we always will be."

He dried her tears with his ever-present handkerchief and Jenny thanked him with a kiss.

He said *you're welcome* with a kiss, and it wasn't until the guests began to giggle and the judge cleared his throat that they returned to the business at hand.

The anticipation that had curled in Jenny's belly all morning turned into something much more exciting. She was glad Matt was holding her hand when the first pain struck. Her knees buckled, but he held fast.

"Are you all right?" he whispered.

Jenny nodded, then looked back to the judge, barely able to keep from breaking into happy laughter.

When they got to the vows, Jenny's hands tightened in Matt's. He looked to her eyes for some sign of indecision and instead found her beaming proudly, looking down as a flood of water poured over the steps like a miniature waterfall.

"Your Honor," Matt said to the judge, "do you think we can hurry things up? I think we're going to have a baby."

In her excitement, Jenny said "I do" twice. After they were pronounced man and wife, Matt shook hands with the judge, John, Greg and Dan and watched as Jenny made her way down a hastily formed reverse receiving line, hugging her friends and tossing out orders on her way to the door.

"Enjoy yourselves. We'll call you later. Save me a piece of wedding cake. And a bottle of champagne, too!"

She waddled to the limo and Mr. Steadman took them to the hospital, where Alexis Elaine was born.

Matt sat on the side of Jenny's bed and used his cell phone to call the wedding guests with the good news.

"Sounds like we're missing one hell of a party," he told her with a smile.

"That's okay. I'm having a pretty good time here." She lifted the baby to her breast for the first time, and Lexie latched on to her mother's nipple like a pro.

Matt dropped a kiss on Jenny's lips, then on Lexie's tiny head. "You know, this parenting thing is going to be hard at times."

"I know," Jenny said, "but anything worth having is worth working for."

He smiled, having thought the same thing a time or two himself. "Even at that, we're bound to make a mistake or two. Maybe even monster ones that hurt and are hard to forgive."

Jenny nodded. She knew he was talking about her parents.

For most of her adult life thoughts of the past had never been far from Jenny's mind, but now they seemed to have evaporated like mist over the valley. She couldn't change what had happened, but she could change the way she felt about it, and find peace within herself.

"I'm so happy today," she said, "I think I can forgive almost anything." She took his hand and kissed the plain gold wedding band she'd placed on his finger. "Maybe it's time we both started over."

Matt agreed with a nod of his head. "If we stick together, we can have it all."

He smiled as he watched Lexie yawn, then settle back to her breakfast. "I'd like to have more children with you, Jenny. A whole houseful, if you're game."

She thought for a moment, then smiled mischievously. "Shall I call Dr. Bentley?"

Matt laughed and kissed her again, brushing the curve of her breast with gentle fingers. "Technology is a wonderful thing, sweetheart. But next time I'd like to do it the old-fashioned way."

* * * * *

SILHOUETTE *Romance*®

presents a brand-new title in

CAROL GRACE's
heartwarming miniseries

Fairy Tale Brides

Cinderellie!

(Silhouette Romance #1775)
Available July 2005
at your favorite retail outlet.

Handsome venture capitalist Jack Martin had the
power to make Ellie Branson's dreams come true.
But could a man who wasn't looking for lasting
love really be her Prince Charming?

Also look for the next Fairy Tale Brides romance:
His Sleeping Beauty
(Silhouette Romance #1792, November 2005)

Visit Silhouette Books at www.eHarlequin.com   SRC

SILHOUETTE *Romance*®

Don't miss a moment of the

Blossom County *Fair*

Where love blooms true!

Rancher Cindy Tucker's challenge? Transforming from tomboy to knockout. Her prize? The cowboy who has haunted her dreams for years. Will he see her in a different light? Find out in:

A Bride for a Blue-Ribbon Cowboy

by JUDY DUARTE

Silhouette Romance #1776
Available July 2005

And the fun continues at the Blossom County Fair!

Flirting with Fireworks (SR #1780)

by TERESA CARPENTER
Available August 2005

The Sheriff Wins a Wife (SR #1784)

by JILL LIMBER
Available September 2005

Her Gypsy Prince (SR #1789)

by CRYSTAL GREEN
Available October 2005

Visit Silhouette Books at www.eHarlequin.com   SRABBRC

If you enjoyed what you just read,
then we've got an offer you can't resist!

Take 2 bestselling love stories FREE!

Plus get a FREE surprise gift!

Clip this page and mail it to Silhouette Reader Service™

IN U.S.A.	IN CANADA
3010 Walden Ave.	P.O. Box 609
P.O. Box 1867	Fort Erie, Ontario
Buffalo, N.Y. 14240-1867	L2A 5X3

YES! Please send me 2 free Silhouette Romance® novels and my free surprise gift. After receiving them, if I don't wish to receive anymore, I can return the shipping statement marked cancel. If I don't cancel, I will receive 4 brand-new novels every month, before they're available in stores! In the U.S.A., bill me at the bargain price of $3.57 plus 25¢ shipping and handling per book and applicable sales tax, if any*. In Canada, bill me at the bargain price of $4.05 plus 25¢ shipping and handling per book and applicable taxes**. That's the complete price and a savings of at least 10% off the cover prices—what a great deal! I understand that accepting the 2 free books and gift places me under no obligation ever to buy any books. I can always return a shipment and cancel at any time. Even if I never buy another book from Silhouette, the 2 free books and gift are mine to keep forever.

210 SDN DZ7L
310 SDN DZ7M

Name	(PLEASE PRINT)	
Address	Apt.#	
City	State/Prov.	Zip/Postal Code

Not valid to current Silhouette Romance® subscribers.

Want to try two free books from another series?
Call 1-800-873-8635 or visit www.morefreebooks.com.

* Terms and prices subject to change without notice. Sales tax applicable in N.Y.
** Canadian residents will be charged applicable provincial taxes and GST.
 All orders subject to approval. Offer limited to one per household.
 ® are registered trademarks owned and used by the trademark owner and or its licensee.

SROM04R   ©2004 Harlequin Enterprises Limited

e**HARLEQUIN**.com

The Ultimate Destination for Women's Fiction

For **FREE online reading**, visit
www.eHarlequin.com now and enjoy:

Online Reads
Read **Daily** and **Weekly** chapters from
our Internet-exclusive stories by your
favorite authors.

Interactive Novels
Cast your vote to help decide how these
stories unfold...then stay tuned!

Quick Reads
For shorter romantic reads, try our
collection of Poems, Toasts, & More!

Online Read Library
Miss one of our online reads?
Come here to catch up!

Reading Groups
Discuss, share and rave with other
community members!

For great reading online,
visit www.eHarlequin.com today!

INTONL04R

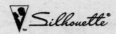

SPECIAL EDITION™

presents a new six-book continuity

MOST LIKELY TO...

Eleven students. One reunion.
And a secret that will change everyone's lives.

On sale July 2005

THE HOMECOMING HERO RETURNS

(SE #1694)

by bestselling author

Joan Elliott Pickart

Former college jock David Westport was convinced he had it all—a beautiful wife, two wonderful kids and a good business in his North End neighborhood. Sandra Westport loved her husband dearly but was positive that he did have one regret—letting her sudden pregnancy derail his chances at a pro baseball career ten years ago. And when a college professor revealed a secret that threw all the good in David's life into shadow, Sandra feared her marriage was over. Could David rebuild his shattered dreams without losing the love of his life?

Don't miss this emotional story—only from Silhouette Books.

Silhouette®

Where love comes alive™

Visit Silhouette Books at www.eHarlequin.com

SSETHHR

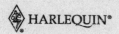 HARLEQUIN®

INTRIGUE

Return to

MCCALLS' MONTANA

this spring
with

B.J. DANIELS

Their land stretched for miles across
the Big Sky state...all of it hard-earned—
none of it negotiable. Could family ties
withstand the weight of lasting legacy?

AMBUSHED!
May

HIGH-CALIBER COWBOY
June

SHOTGUN SURRENDER
July

Available wherever Harlequin Books are sold.

www.eHarlequin.com   HIA